"Melody, it's s_____ ____—"

Melody interrup_____ the house. "I need y____

Gracie furrowed her eyebrows as she shut the door. "Okay. Is something wrong?"

Wyatt squealed from inside his playpen and reached up to Melody. Unable to withstand any fussing from that precious boy, Melody scooped him up into her arms. He immediately reached for her hair. "Nothing's wrong. I've agreed to do Bible study with Drew, but just as friends."

"Okay?" Gracie still looked confused.

"And I want to do something about my hair."

"What's wrong with your hair? It's gorgeous."

Warmth trailed up her neck. "I mean I don't want to wear it up in a ponytail, and I don't know what to do with it."

Gracie squinted and cocked her head. "I thought you were going to be just friends."

Melody huffed and shifted Wyatt to her other hip. "We are." She nestled her nose into the baby's neck, avoiding eye contact with her friend. "I just want to look a little prettier."

Gracie lifted her eyebrows and slowly nodded her head. "I see."

Melody rolled her eyes. "I'm not ready for Drew to be my boyfriend, but when I am ready—"

"You want Drew to be your boyfriend."

JENNIFER JOHNSON and her unbelievably supportive husband, Albert, are happily married and raising Brooke, Hayley, and Allie, the three cutest young ladies on the planet. Besides being a middle school teacher, Jennifer loves to read, write, and chauffeur her girls. She is a member of the American Christian Fiction Writers. Blessed beyond measure, Jennifer hopes to always think like a child—bigger than imaginable and with complete faith. Send her a note at jenwrites4god@bellsouth.net.

Books by Jennifer Johnson

HEARTSONG PRESENTS
HP725—By His Hand
HP738—Picket Fence Pursuit
HP766—Pursuing the Goal
HP802—In Pursuit of Peace
HP866—Finding Home
HP882—For Better or Worse
HP901—Gaining Love
HP920—Maid to Love

Betting on Love

Jennifer Johnson

Heartsong Presents

To New Hope Baptist Church in Versailles, Kentucky. You have been Albert's and my church family since we were newlyweds (as you know, we were still babies ourselves). You have loved us through all of life's ups and downs. I am so thankful to know each and every one of you. I love you all so much. God is so good!

A note from the Author:
I love to hear from my readers! You may correspond with me by writing:

Jennifer Johnson
Author Relations
PO Box 721
Uhrichsville, OH 44683

ISBN 978-1-61626-230-3

BETTING ON LOVE

Scripture taken from the Holy Bible, New International Version®. niv®. Copyright © 1973, 1978, 1984 by International Bible Society. Used by permission of Zondervan. All rights reserved.

All of the characters and events in this book are fictitious. Any resemblance to actual persons, living or dead, or to actual events is purely coincidental.

Our mission is to publish and distribute inspirational products offering exceptional value and biblical encouragement to the masses.

one

Drew Wilson stared at his sister's bridesmaid. The girl was entirely too cute to be a diesel mechanic. He gulped down the last of his punch in an attempt to stave off the taste of the green ice cream and lemon-lime drink. *Who would have thought up such a disgusting mixture, and why does everyone think they have to have it at their wedding?* He scraped his tongue against the roof of his mouth, trying not to gag at the aftertaste.

Looking back at Melody Markwell, he took in how the silver, shiny dress hugged her body in a way that he was sure it could never hug any other diesel mechanic he'd ever known. And the pinky purple belt thing around her waist—what was it his sister had called it? He chewed the inside of his jaw. *A raspberry-colored sash.* Not only did the silky strip wrap around her skinny waist in the most froufrou bow he'd ever seen, but it also matched the color of her lips, which were a bit too plump in his opinion.

And her hair—well it rolled all the way down her back like a mud-covered hill on a wet spring afternoon after he and his buddies had four wheeled up and down until their tanks were dry. He cocked his head. Okay, he had to admit her hair looked quite a bit prettier than a muddy hill, which was proof enough that the woman couldn't really be a diesel mechanic. At least not one of any account.

That national certification license she liked to spout off about didn't mean anything, even if he didn't know anyone in town who had one.

He tossed the clear plastic cup into the trash can. Sucking in his breath, he stepped toward the woman who grated on his nerves something fierce. Of course, the dark-haired nuisance just had to be standing close to his newly married sister, Addy, and her husband—one of Drew's best friends—Nick, as well as several of their friends.

"It sounds like it's just a spark plug." Melody's voice lifted through the air like a little bird. More proof that she couldn't be any kind of mechanic. "Tomorrow I'll come out and give it a check. Won't take me five minutes to fix."

Drew bit back the urge to gag. The woman thought she knew everything about everything.

"I'd appreciate it," Gracie, Addy's best friend, answered. "Wyatt just doesn't know much about vehicles. We usually ask Drew, but he's always so busy. . . ."

Drew cleared his throat. "Don't ever hesitate to ask me. It's no trouble for *me* to fix your car." He knew he'd emphasized the *me* a bit too much, but he didn't care. Melody didn't need to fix his friends' vehicles. He'd been helping them just fine for years.

Gracie jumped and placed her hand on her chest as she turned toward him. "Drew, you scared the life out of me. I didn't know you were there."

He looked at Melody Markwell, the woman who'd walked into his town thinking she could do everything from helping his sister organize a wedding to fixing every vehicle in the county. Not that he minded a self-reliant woman. He'd been raised by a strong mother and alongside an independent sister, but this Melody had some kind of chip on her shoulder. And she was too cute. And she invaded his thoughts at the oddest moments. And he didn't like that one bit.

Melody squinted and glared at him. He smirked when she lifted her little chin up at him. "I'm sure *I* can figure it out without a problem."

Noting the challenge in her tone, he straightened his shoulders and crossed his arms in front of his chest as he peered down at the slip of a woman. "I guess we'll have to wait and see."

Melody opened her mouth, but the sound of someone clapping stopped her from making any kind of retort. He looked over and saw his mother wave her hands in animated anticipation as everyone turned their attention her way. A broad smile lit up her face, and he knew she and Nick's mom, who had been best friends all their lives, were ecstatic about the union of their children. "It's time to cut the cake."

Drew nodded at Melody and Gracie then made his way to his buddy Mike, who stood in the far corner. The whole day was making him sick to his stomach. Sure, he was glad to see his sister so happy, and he liked that the fellow she snagged was not only a solid Christian but also one of his best friends. But getting all dressed up in a monkey suit just to stand around choking down the frothy punch—he yanked at the collar of his shirt—it just seemed to be a waste of the time he could have spent working on the farm.

He most definitely liked beating Nick at the no-women bet he, Wyatt, Mike, and Nick had made several years before. After watching another buddy succumb to a life of working long hours only to go home to a needy wife and whiny kids, the four of them had made a bet that none of them wanted to lose: The first three to get married would have to help plan and pay for the wedding of the guy who waited the longest. Something none of them intended to take part in.

With Wyatt and Nick having already given over to the female wiles, Drew was a sure win. Mike was a great guy, but he couldn't win a bet unless the rest of them handed the prize over to him. And Drew had never been one to hand a win over to anyone.

Drew grabbed Mike's hand in a firm shake. "How's it going?"

"Just standing here watching another one of us get reeled in."

Drew glanced at his sister and Nick. She had just shoved an oversized piece of cake into his face. Nick gripped both her hands in one of his and held them in the air while he rubbed his cake-covered face against her cheek. Drew wrinkled his nose. Seeing his friend and his sister so lovey-dovey made his stomach turn.

He looked back at Mike, two years his junior, and guffawed at the horrified expression on his face. He patted Mike's shoulder. "Well, we both know you're next to fall."

Mike shrugged off Drew's palm. "I don't know about that. I have just as many prospects as you." He lifted his hand and connected his index finger to his thumb to make a zero.

Drew blew out a breath. "Are you kidding? You and Lacy have been making moon eyes at each other for nearly two years."

Mike's face reddened, and he stammered as he did every time someone said something that was a bit too close to the truth. "We have not." He nodded toward Melody Markwell.

"What about that gal over there? Nick's cousin? She seemed to get under your skin fast enough."

Drew snorted. "You said it. The woman gets under my skin like a tick burrowing its head into flesh so it can suck out the blood of its victim." He shook his head and almost chuckled at how true the analogy was. "No. I don't believe that gal's a threat to my bachelorhood."

"How 'bout Terri Fletcher?" Mike motioned toward the tall, thin girl who stood close to Drew's mother. Terri had always reminded Drew of Olive Oyl from the old Popeye cartoons. Not only was she almost as tall as Drew and as thick as a blade of grass, but she even wore her black hair tied in a knot most of the time. "She's had her sights set on you since the ninth grade," Mike said.

Drew flared his nostrils. The woman had been quite the nemesis to him throughout high school and a few years following. That is, until he'd let her know in direct terms that he was in no way interested in pursuing romantic notions with her or anyone. "I don't suppose I've got my sights set on Terri either."

Mike shrugged. "I guess we'll wait and see."

Drew turned his attention back to Nick and Addy. Melody walked up to his sister and handed her another napkin to wipe the cake off her face. The sunlight from the window seemed to dance around Melody, probably from the diamond-looking thingies she'd stuck all over the top of her head.

He exhaled a sigh of disgust. The woman looked downright adorable. Even prettier than a newborn fawn. The truth of it grated Drew's nerves and twisted something on the inside. He didn't want to think about what that something was.

❧

Melody folded the last raspberry-colored tablecloth and laid it in the box Addy's mother had given her. Laughter and squeals from children romping on the playground seeped through the windows and door, tempting her to slip off the rhinestone-studded heels and join them.

She peered around the room. Addy and Nick's wedding party and family had spent the last few hours cleaning up after the ceremony. The sanctuary and fellowship hall were undecorated and freshly scoured, ready for Sunday services the next morning. Warmth crept up her neck and cheeks when she remembered the look of longing in both Nick's and Addy's eyes as they headed for their first evening as husband and wife to the cabin he'd built.

Peals of laughter filled the room again, and Melody bit her bottom lip. She knew it wouldn't be proper to roughhouse with a bunch of kids in her fancy silver bridesmaid dress. Despite how much fun she'd had getting all dolled up for her cousin's and Addy's big day, she longed to let down her hair, both literally and figuratively, and just have a good time in the spring sunshine. She wondered how long it would take her to get the rhinestone twirly things out of her hair. Aunt Renee would have to help her when they got back to the house.

She looked out the window, watching as the children struggled to push the merry-go-round fast enough. She smiled at the determined expression of a little guy who couldn't have been more than five.

Kentucky was especially beautiful in the spring when the dogwood and honeysuckle, daylilies, tulips, and irises bloomed to breathtaking perfection. This May sky didn't contain even a trace of the showers that so often dripped, sprinkled, and even poured during the fifth month of the year in the Bluegrass State. Today, the sun smiled upon River Run, and the breeze blew with just the slightest kiss to the cheek.

Melody couldn't stand it any longer. She kicked off her shoes, picked them up, then raced out the back door. After dropping the heels on the picnic table, she scooped up a handful of her dress and made her way to the merry-go-round. "You want me to push you?"

"Yeah!" The little boy she'd been watching jumped onto the merry-go-round and wrapped his legs and arms around one of the metal bars. She knew he was Dana's—the church custodian's—great-grandson, but she couldn't remember the boy's name.

Melody nodded to the two redheaded girls, Beth and Becca, twin granddaughters of Sherri, the soloist in the wedding. Melody figured they were probably about the same age as the boy. "You ready?"

The girls cheered and giggled as they locked their arms around the bar and each other.

"Okay. Here I go." In an attempt to keep her dress as clean as possible, she continued to grip the satiny material with her left hand and pushed bar after bar with her right.

The kids squealed with delight, and before Melody had a chance to think through her actions, she hopped onto the merry-go-round with them. The wind felt amazing whipping through her hair, and she bellowed out along with the children. Losing her grip on the bar, she started to slip, and the little guy grabbed hold of her arm. "I got ya," he said. His face grimaced as he held tight to her arm.

She smiled at the youngster. "Thanks, buddy." It was nice to see a boy who was so chivalrous. Her experience with the male gender had been that most of them didn't even begin to have that quality.

As the merry-go-round started to slow down, a figure in the parking lot caught her gaze. Her cheeks warmed when she was able to make out the confused expression on Addy's brother's face. Embarrassment welled in her chest at how silly she must appear. A grown woman should never jump and scream on a merry-go-round in a satin bridesmaid dress. And to do so in front of Drew Wilson only made matters worse. *That man knows how to get under my skin like no one I've ever known before.*

Lifting her chin, Melody determined she would not allow the man to make her feel uncomfortable, inferior, or whatever it was she felt every time she was around him. She hopped up and brushed the dirt and wrinkles from the shiny dress.

"Push us again!" one of the twins squealed.

Melody smiled down at them, noting how much they looked like their grandmother. "I'm afraid I need to help the grown-ups finish packing things into the cars."

"Ah," the girls groaned.

The little guy jumped off and lifted his left hand in the air as if to stop traffic. "It's okay." He grabbed the bar with his right hand. "I'll push."

Melody lifted her hand to high-five the child. "Thanks, buddy."

If she ever had a son, she would teach him to be as kind to girls as this little one was. She sighed. She loved children, but there was no way she'd ever have a son to raise. She wasn't willing to date, let alone marry, any man.

The boy smacked her hand then focused back on the merry-go-round. Melody turned back toward Drew. She noted the humor etched on his expression and couldn't decipher if he was inwardly laughing at her or amused by her. She didn't particularly want him to be either. The man had been nothing but a half-empty glass and a condescending chauvinist since she arrived in River Run. He'd made it abundantly clear he didn't believe women could do mechanic work as well as men. Given the chance, she'd have no problem showing him different. She averted her gaze and walked past him.

"Melody."

She stopped when he said her name. There was no telling what smart-aleck comment he would have to say about her playing on the merry-go-round with the kids. She turned and looked at him, ready to verbally spar in any way necessary.

"Mom's grilling hamburgers and hot dogs for all of us. She already has everything ready." He looked away from her, and she wondered why he seemed suddenly uncomfortable. "I'm supposed to tell you to come."

"I was planning on it."

"Did he tell you we're gonna play cornhole, too?" Mike walked up beside Drew and patted his shoulder. "The only person who's ever beat Drew just left on his honeymoon."

Her heart filled with excitement, and the thought of beating Drew Wilson at the game sent it to pounding. "I love cornhole. I haven't played in ages."

Mike raised one eyebrow. "You any good?"

Teasing, Melody blew on her knuckles then brushed her

shoulder. "Back home I was town champion two years in a row."

Drew grunted and rolled his eyes.

Fire blazed through Melody's veins at the man's pompous attitude. She wished she'd known they'd be playing cornhole. She'd have practiced a bit to ensure she whipped up on Drew Wilson. The man desperately needed to be knocked down a few pegs. "Maybe you and I will have a chance to play, Drew."

He gazed back at her. Challenge lit his eyes. "I'm sure we will."

❧

Melody couldn't help but watch Drew as he glowered in the far corner of his family living room. Pride puffed up her chest and filled her gut. So much so, she couldn't even finish the hot dog she'd started eating.

Gracie sat beside Melody. Her plate was filled with a loaded grilled hamburger; potato salad made by Drew's mom, Amanda; and her aunt Renee's coleslaw. The food was delicious, and Melody wished she had room in her stomach to finish off her plate.

"Where's that big boy of yours?" Melody asked.

Gracie pointed her fork toward Wyatt, who was making his way to Drew and Mike. "His dad's letting me eat first."

"I would have held him while you ate."

"You need to eat, too." She took a bite of potato salad then wiped her mouth with a napkin. "Besides, Drew probably needs cheering up after you whipped him twice at cornhole."

Indescribable satisfaction swelled within her. "That man needed to be knocked down a few notches. He's entirely too cocky."

Gracie laughed and swatted her hand. "Aw, Drew's a

great guy. He just always wins at everything. After a while, you can't blame the guy for simply expecting it."

Melody remembered the mixed expression of shock and horror on Drew's face when she sank the corn kernel–filled beanbag into the hole for her first win. "Then I'm glad I could help him get a taste of losing."

Gracie lifted her fork in the air and shook it back and forth. "Be careful, Melody. You know what the Bible says—pride comes before a fall."

Melody tried not to roll her eyes. She didn't know what the Bible said, and she really didn't care, either. It had been abundantly clear in the months she'd spent living with her aunt and uncle that they were Holy Rollers. Evidently, years before, when her mom and dad were still married, before her dad skipped out on them, her mom had been religious as well. But Melody had very few remembrances of church or the Bible or God. Her mom worked too hard and too many hours to worry about spending time with Melody, let alone fret about going to church. Her mom had given up on God and everything else when her dad left, so He must not be that great.

Melody pointed toward Drew. "You saw how the overgrown boy acted. He practically stomped off after I beat him the second time. He hasn't even so much as looked at me since. No 'good game,' 'congratulations,' or anything."

Gracie pushed a stray strand of blond hair behind her ear. Melody felt a niggling of jealousy at Gracie's beautiful light hair, eyes, and complexion. Everything about the woman was feminine and dainty. Though she was on the short side and she had a small frame, Melody felt like a dark-haired, dark-eyed workhorse beside her new friend. "He has definitely been acting strange the last few months. Probably because his little sister just married one of his best friends."

"Or maybe he's just a male chauvinist pig."

Gracie frowned. "You have Drew pegged wrong. He's a good Christian man." She took a drink of her sweet tea. "By the way, are you planning to come to church tomorrow?"

Melody wrinkled her nose. Church seemed to be all everyone in this town ever talked about. She'd agreed to go a few times with her aunt and uncle, but she didn't really care much for it. All the preacher ever talked about was having a personal relationship with the Lord. Well, she'd done just fine without that personal relationship for twenty-four years. Why would she all of a sudden have to have it now? "I don't know."

"Afterward, you could come over for lunch then take a look at our car."

Melody squinted. "I thought Christians were supposed to rest on Sunday."

Gracie leaned toward her. "Will I be able to convince you to come to church if I promise you can look at my car?"

Melody grinned at Gracie's sneaky motives. "Possibly."

Gracie smacked her leg. "Then by all means, after church you can come look at my car."

Melody shook her head. Since she'd moved to River Run, she'd been working as much as she could to build up her name as a trustworthy mechanic in the area, and Gracie knew she'd like to have the good word of the owner of the town's hardware store. "Fine. I'll be there."

two

Drew grabbed the supplies for the house he was going to build then walked up to the counter of the hardware store. In just a few more days he'd have the ground leveled; then he and his friends could start working on the foundation. Having bought the land from his dad several years before, Drew had finally saved enough money to build a modest home.

After fixing up the cabin Nick had built on his land, Drew had no doubt he and his friends had the know-how to build a small home. Unlike Nick, Drew wasn't in a rush. They could work on it a bit at a time until it was done. He'd have his own place and no debt. He could use his money as God guided instead of forking it all over to a bank.

"This all you need?" Wyatt scanned the first item.

Drew nodded. "For now anyway."

Wyatt picked up the spark plug and furrowed his eyebrows. "What's this for?"

"The dump truck. I'm pretty sure that's all that's wrong with her."

"Is it broken or just not running well?"

"Won't start up like it should."

"Are you sure it's just a spark plug? Melody came over to the house yesterday after church, and she fixed Gracie's car in no time flat. I was sure it was—"

Drew lifted his hand as he peered at his friend. "I believe

I know a bit more about vehicles than you."

Wyatt raised his hands in surrender. "Hey, don't be so defensive, man. I wasn't insulting your abilities. I was just saying Melody really seems to know what she's talking about—"

Drew clenched his hand then pounded the counter with the side of his fist. "And you don't think I do?"

"What is the matter with you, Drew? Why does she get on your nerves so bad?"

Drew thought of Melody in the long silver dress she wore as Addy's bridesmaid. She'd looked amazing with the sides of her thick, dark hair tied in a knot at the back of her head and the rest of it flowing in long curls down her back. Her dark eyes held such depth and mystery. When she walked down the aisle, for a moment, Drew nearly lost his breath.

Then he'd watched her play with the kids on the merry-go-round. Her expression and body language had been of complete freedom and bliss. Her laughter rang through the breeze with the children's, and he'd found himself again drawn to her as he'd never been drawn to a woman before.

Then she'd challenged him to cornhole. The Melody he'd seen when she first arrived in River Run exposed herself. Melody couldn't simply have fun with the game. She had to win. She had to gloat. Sure, the gloating had only come from her expression, not her lips. Still, Drew had noted it all the same.

She was the same way when it came to mechanics. She had to prove to everyone that she was the best, that they should trust their transportation to her and no one else. And after years of looking after the vehicles of his family and friends, he took offense to her waltzing into River Run and stomping all over his toes.

Drew finally looked at Wyatt. "The woman thinks she knows everything."

"You mean about vehicles?"

Drew nodded his head. "That's one thing she thinks she knows it all about."

Wyatt leaned forward against the counter. "She *is* a nationally certified diesel mechanic."

Drew rolled his eyes. "Who cares?"

"And she's good."

"A lot of people are good. I'm good."

Wyatt lifted one eyebrow. "Are you jealous of a *girl*, Drew Wilson?"

Drew folded his arms across his chest and growled. "Do I need to whip some sense into you? It's been a few years since I've done it, but you know I can. Of course I'm not jealous of her. It's her cocky attitude that gets on my nerves."

"She did beat you at cornhole." Wyatt's mouth curved upward just a tad on the left side, and Drew felt a real urge to punch his friend in the face. Wyatt lifted two fingers in the air. "Twice."

Anger boiled within Drew, and he pointed his finger at Wyatt. "Now, look here. . ."

Wyatt backed away from the counter. "Actually, you two are a whole lot alike. You're both so stinkin' competitive. Have to be the best at everything. But you're a Christian, and she's not."

Drew's fury started to simmer. He knew Melody wasn't a Christian. Addy had prayed for her every night at the dinner table before she and Nick got married.

Wyatt continued. "Gracie prays for her constantly. She really likes Melody, but the woman's got some kind of wall all built up around her. She doesn't want to let anyone in. Not even Gracie, and you know how easy it is for people to open up to Gracie."

Drew blew out a long breath. "Addy feels the same way. Nick said Melody was raised by her mom, just the two of them. I guess her mom had to work a lot of hours. Nick said he thought things were kind of hard for Melody."

Anger washed across Wyatt's face as he handed the receipt to Drew. "As long as I have breath in this body, I'll do everything I can to take care of Gracie and our son. I'd never leave her to fend for herself. I don't understand a man who could do that."

Sobered and feeling thankful for his mother and father, Drew grabbed his bag off the counter. "I've got to head on over to the homesite. I'll talk to you later."

His heart felt heavy as he made his way back to his truck. He loved the Lord with all his heart, soul, mind, and strength. At least he'd always believed he did. Sure, he knew he was a bit competitive and could be a bit mule headed at times. He wasn't perfect, but he always wanted to be sensitive to God's guiding and what God wanted from him.

After turning the ignition, he prayed silently as he started down the road. *God, Wyatt's right. I have been defensive when it comes to Melody. I don't know what it is about her that rubs me the wrong way. Forgive me, Lord. Help me be a better witness for You.*

He slammed his brakes when a small mutt ran into the middle of the road. The contents of the hardware bag fell out onto the floor of the truck. He saw the spark plugs, and an idea popped into his head.

He groaned as he lifted his cap off his head, wiped the sweat off his brow with the back of his hand, then placed the cap back on. "God, isn't there some other way?"

His heart felt as if it had been nudged again, and Drew cringed as he took the cell phone out of his pocket. "God, I wouldn't do this for anyone but You."

৯

Hands filled with various vegetable seedlings, Melody followed her aunt Renee outside to the newly tilled garden. She felt like a fish out of water helping her aunt with plants and flowers. Melody knew everything there was to know about cleaning a house, doing laundry, and even fixing all kinds of things from televisions to microwaves to car engines, but she'd had absolutely no experience messing with Mother Nature.

"Okay, Melody." Aunt Renee set down the plants then pointed to the right side of the huge garden area. Melody followed her lead and placed her plants on the ground. "I'm going to have you put the cucumbers over there. They need plenty of room to spread out."

Melody nodded. "Okay. Which ones are the cucumbers?"

Aunt Renee picked up a tray with six plants. She handed them to Melody with a wry grin. "The ones with the picture of a cucumber on the tag."

"Make fun of me all you want, Aunt Renee." Melody smiled as she gently touched the dainty green leaves on the plants. "You're the crazy one for letting me touch these poor things."

"You'll be fine." She handed her a small shovel. Melody had never seen one so small. It was kind of cute. "Plant them about a foot apart."

Melody nodded. She headed to her spot then surveyed the area where she was to plant the cucumbers. A foot apart seemed awfully far, but she didn't know anything about gardening, so she'd have to trust her aunt.

Melody knelt down and touched the soft earth. It actually felt nice and cool and squishy between her fingers. Her aunt had fussed all morning about getting the garden out about a week and a half later than she normally did, but Nick and Addy's wedding had taken precedence over the garden.

Might as well get to it, Melody chided herself. She wasn't sure how deep to dig. She glanced over at her aunt, who appeared quite busy with what Melody believed were the tomato plants—although she had no idea why her aunt was placing circular wire contraptions over the small plants.

She shrugged. If the plants had to be a foot away from each other, they probably needed to be around a foot deep. She gazed at the small plants. But the cucumber seedlings were probably only six inches tall at the most.

Just do it. If I can fix an engine, I can plant a cucumber.

She stuck the small trowel into the earth and shoveled out several shovelfuls of dirt. Once she had a good-sized mound beside the hole, she firmly stuck the plant inside then covered most of it with the mound.

I would say the plants need plenty of water, so I'll build the dirt up around the plant; that way it will kind of be like a bowl to catch the rain.

Still unsure if she'd planted it deep enough, she looked at the small bit of cucumber plant that stuck out from the circular hole she'd created. She had no idea if it looked right or not. Peering over at her aunt, she watched her put another wire contraption over another plant. Blowing out her breath, Melody decided it was good enough and started a hole for the next plant.

Once she'd finished three more plants, she realized a shadow fell over her. She looked up to find Aunt Renee standing over her with her hands on her hips.

"Melody, what are you doing?" Her aunt's voice was calm and smooth.

Melody furrowed her eyebrows, unable to see her aunt's expression because of the sunlight. "I'm planting cucumbers."

"Are you planting them or burying them?"

Melody cupped her hand over her eyebrows trying to shield the sun. "What do you mean?"

A smile bowed Aunt Renee's lips, and she turned toward the other side of the garden. "Roy, come over here. You gotta see this."

Melody watched as her uncle walked toward them. She looked down at the cucumber plants, trying to figure out what her aunt thought was so humorous. She'd planted them a foot apart. She'd stuck them in the ground, even made kind of a bowl shape around them allowing them plenty of opportunity to hold water. A little bit of each plant stuck up from the top.

She stood and wiped her hands on her hips while her uncle made his way beside them. An obnoxious laugh snorted from Uncle Roy's mouth when he looked at her plants. "Melody, what were you thinking?"

She crossed her arms in front of her chest, trying not to feel foolish or defensive. "What?"

Aunt Renee bent down and pulled the first plant out of its crater. She filled most of the hole then gently placed the seedling into a much smaller hole and pushed dirt around it. "The plants need to be closer to the top to get the sunlight. And you want the dirt to go downward, away from the plant. The plants would drown the other way around."

"I told you I don't know what I'm doing." Melody tried to smile as she spoke through gritted teeth. She tried to swallow back her embarrassment as she thought of the many times her mother had chided her about her need to do everything right the first time—her need for perfection.

"You're doing fine. You're learning. You gave us a good laugh this morning." Uncle Roy patted her back. "Remember the last time you got a good laugh from me."

Melody's mind replayed the time Uncle Roy had tried to fix his muffler with wire and duct tape. She'd been both appalled and tickled by the mess he'd made of the poor car part. She grinned. "I sure do."

Aunt Renee shook her head, obviously remembering as well. She pointed to the buried cucumber plants. "Go ahead and fix those. You know how to do it now."

Melody nodded and bent down to her work as her aunt and uncle walked back to their spots in the garden. Her cell phone vibrated in her pocket. Flustered, she tried to wipe as much dirt as possible onto her jean shorts then dug into her pocket for the phone. She pulled it out and pressed the TALK button. "Hello."

Silence. She pulled it away from her ear to see if she'd lost the connection. She didn't recognize the number, but they were still connected. She put it back to her ear. "Hello," she tried again.

The caller cleared his throat. "Hello, Melody?"

She pulled the phone away from her ear to look at the number again. She furrowed her brows. The caller sounded an awful lot like Addy's brother, Drew. But surely he'd be the last person on the planet to call her. She placed the phone back against her ear. "Yes, this is she."

The caller cleared his throat again. "Umm. This is Drew—Addy's brother."

A sudden panic gripped her heart. The only reason he'd call her was if something happened to Addy or to Nick. Maybe he'd called her because he didn't know how to tell Uncle Roy and Aunt Renee that something happened. "What's wrong? Did something happen to Addy and Nick?"

"What?" He sounded confused. "No. No. As far as I know they're fine. Haven't heard from them, but then I wouldn't expect to." He chuckled then stopped. "I need to ask a favor of you."

Suspicion filled her gut. What would Drew Wilson want from her? A rematch at cornhole? To try to make her look silly? He'd made it abundantly obvious he thought she was just a silly little woman. Pride swelled within her, and a slow grin formed on her lips. But she'd proven herself better than him in every way he'd challenged her.

"Did you hear me? I need your help," he said.

"Okay. What do you need?"

"The dump truck I'm using. It doesn't start up well. Sometimes I can't get her going at all. I was wondering if you'd come look at it."

Melody squinted. "You can't fix it yourself?"

"I need your help."

Even over the phone, she could tell saying those four words had taken a lot out of him. And even though she felt he was probably up to something, Melody was itching to have the opportunity to work on some heavy machinery. "Okay. I'll come over after lunch. Your house, right?"

"Actually, it's at my homesite. I'm building my own house. I'll meet you at my parents' house and bring you on out here."

"Okay." Melody clicked the phone off. Bending down she tried to focus on the cucumber plants once more. Her heartbeat sped up, and a knot twisted in her gut. It was kind of weird. She'd never been so excited to see an oversized truck.

three

Melody admired Kentucky's idyllic scenery as she followed behind Drew's pickup. He'd invited her to ride along with him, but she'd insisted she might need the tools packed in the back of her truck. Now she could drink in the rolling grass-covered hills dotted with trees of various kinds and sizes. Cattle grazed on the right side of the road, and Melody smiled as two calves chased each other in the field.

The old gravel road took them past a slightly swollen, rolling creek. She wondered about the crawdads that most definitely lived within it, reminiscing about a time when she and some friends spent an afternoon fishing for the small lobsterlike critters.

The ride was peaceful, serene. It was beautiful, awe inspiring. She thrilled at the idea of living in such a place. Though she'd been raised in a small town, her mother could only afford a small apartment in town. She'd relished the times she'd been able to romp the countryside with friends, always longing to live close to Mother Nature and away from people. People didn't treat each other right. They lied. They abandoned. They mistreated. It was one of the reasons she loved machines so much. She didn't need someone else to help her work on one. It was a solo activity, most of the time anyway. The road grew narrower and less traveled. For a moment, the trees seemed to grow thicker around them. Then they opened up into a beautiful cleared-out field.

Melody took in the machinery, spying the dump truck she assumed she was to look at. She noted the flags marking the spot of Drew's future home. Just beyond the markings, she saw a good-sized pond. He'd practically be able to cast a line off his back porch. The idea of it made her smile.

Drew stopped his truck then hopped out. Melody followed his lead. He swiped his hand across the expanse of the place. Pride radiated from him. "Here it is." He looked down at her, and Melody was surprised that his gaze held a hint of need for approval.

She swallowed the knot in her throat. It was the first time she'd noted any kind of vulnerability in Drew, and if she could allow herself to be honest with him, she'd tell him how amazing she thought the place would be. Instead her defenses took control, and her words came out flat and elusive. "It's nice."

A trace of hurt flashed across his expression. He nodded toward the dump truck. "There it is. Let's go take a look."

Without a backward glance, he walked toward the machine. Melody inwardly chided herself. He'd wanted her to praise the land, and it was worthy of a few accolades. The place was amazing.

She could just picture a small ranch home—brick or log, she wasn't sure which she would picture. Either would be beautiful. A full front porch would extend the length of the house with a porch swing on both sides. She wondered if he'd put his bedroom in the back of the house, so he could build a deck off it so that he could sit outside his own bedroom and look out over the pond.

She shook her head. What was she thinking? She had no business thinking about how Drew Wilson should set up his house. She didn't even like the man. She didn't like any man. Well, except Uncle Roy. He'd proven to be different than any other man she'd ever known.

"Let me show you what she's doing." She watched as Drew hopped up into the cab of the dump truck. He shoved in the key and turned the ignition. The truck groaned and whined before she finally puttered to life. He turned it off and started it again. This time the machine jumped to a quick start.

Drew turned it off then hopped back out of the truck. "Well, that's what she's doing. One time she'll start right up. The next time she whines and carries on until she finally decides to run. Occasionally, she just won't start at all."

Melody nodded. "Oil's good? Filter's good?"

"Yes."

"What about the starter?"

"It should be fine. Replaced a little over six months ago."

Melody noted he'd had trouble answering the second question. She sneaked a peek at Drew. It was obvious asking for her help was hard on his ego. "Okay. Let's have a look inside."

Melody looked around the engine. It needed some new spark plugs, but that wouldn't cause her to vary the way she started up as much as Drew was describing. Melody hopped into the cab and examined the ignition. The problem was as obvious as the nose on her face. He needed to change the plugs and put in a new ignition.

She looked at Drew. His hands were shoved down deep into his jeans pockets. A scowl wrapped his features. Not only was he a self-proclaimed Mr. Handyman, but many people around town agreed with his belief and sought him out for help with their stuff. There was no way he could have missed what was wrong with this truck. The problem was too simple. He was just acting like he didn't know what was wrong. But why?

Gazing out at his property, she realized something she hadn't thought of before. They were alone. Way back in the heart of the Bluegrass State, and they were completely and utterly alone.

Her chest tightened, and her heart raced as she remembered running through the county park back at her own stomping grounds. At fourteen, she'd only wanted to practice for the high school cross-country team. She'd discovered running long distances took her mind off her worries of her mom having to work so hard to provide for them. She didn't have to think about how her mom rarely talked to her when she was home, almost ignoring her completely. It allowed her to breathe in the clean air and blow out the constant concerns and stresses and worries.

Then the man grabbed her. He seemed to have come from nowhere and everywhere all at the same time. She felt his strong, large hand wrapped around the top of her arm, so tight she thought her bone would crack. His breath smelled of cigarettes, strong and stale.

She shook the thought away. She would not allow herself to go there. She'd put that behind her, never to be thought of or relived again. She wouldn't allow it now.

After hopping down out of the cab, she stared at Drew as she straightened her shoulders and crossed her arms in front of her chest. "Why did you ask me to come out here?"

A puzzled expression wrapped his face. "I think the reason is obvious." He pointed to the truck.

She squinted at him. "Really? It's not so obvious to me

why you asked me here. What *is* obvious is what's wrong with the truck. It's an easy fix." She pointed her finger at his chest. "And you and I both know you know how to fix it."

His face flamed red, but Melody knew she'd hit him right between the eyes. He did know how to fix that truck. He'd brought her out for a different reason. Knowing men as she did, she believed it couldn't be an honorable one.

Balling her fists, she broadened her stance, preparing herself for a physical battle if the need arose. She'd taken self-defense, and she now knew how to take care of herself. "So, why would you bring me all the way out here—all alone?"

Drew looked at the expanse of his place once more then peered back at her. Realization at what she was asking seemed to dawn on him, and he took a few steps back shaking his hands in front of his chest. "No way."

Melody cocked her head. "Well, then explain."

Drew's expression turned grim, and he set his jaw. "Don't flatter yourself, Melody. I only wanted help with my truck."

Taken aback by his words, she sucked in her breath. Was he insulting her? Was he saying he was too good for her? Of the all the arrogant, egotistical men—

He spoke again. "I take offense at what you're thinking. You need to go on home."

Feeling as if she'd been sucker punched, Melody tried to lift her chin. She could feel the start of tears forming in her eyes. In less time than a cow can swish her tail, she'd gone from fearing he'd try to take advantage of her to feeling unwanted, unworthy, and unattractive. "I'd still like to know why you asked me here."

"Obviously, you wouldn't understand. Go home." Drew turned and walked toward his truck.

Without hesitation Melody hopped into her own pickup, started it, and headed down the gravel road toward the main road. The unwanted tears she'd been able to hold at bay now streamed freely down her face. She felt perplexed that he'd asked her help for something so simple. Even more so, she was an idiot. A foolish woman. How could she have been worried and ready to fight if Drew had intended to get her alone, and then offended that he had no desire to be alone with her?

&

Drew couldn't remember the last time he'd been so insulted. Melody actually believed he'd driven her out to his place to take advantage of her. He fumed as he grabbed the spark plugs he'd bought for the dump truck out of the cab of his pickup.

Sure, he'd called for her help, and yes, he did know how to fix the dump truck. He looked heavenward. "But God, that's what I thought You wanted me to do. I know the woman doesn't know You, and I know she and I don't always see eye to eye on most things."

He shrugged his shoulders then grabbed his toolbox out of the bed of the pickup. "Okay, we have yet to see eye to eye on anything. But still, I thought You were telling me to call her out here—make her feel needed or wanted or whatever it is that silly woman needs. I just wanted to be a good witness."

You can't do that by fibbing. His spirit spoke within his heart.

He let out a long sigh. "I know."

With a heavy heart, he changed the spark plugs in the truck. Though he hated to admit it, his heart ached a bit that she hadn't been more excited about his homesite. Every bit a country girl, he thought she might swoon over the pond that made up much of his backyard.

He growled at his thinking as he tightened the spark plugs. What did he care what she thought? She drove him to insanity. Always having to win everything. Always having to prove herself to everyone.

"Actually, you two are a whole lot alike. You're both so stinkin' competitive. Have to be the best at everything. But you're a Christian, and she's not." Wyatt's words flooded his mind anew.

She was a lot like him. He knew she was. Which also meant she wouldn't back down from anybody for any reason. She thought he had tried to hoodoo her out here to fix his dump truck. She'd thought he'd had an ulterior motive.

Well, the truth was he did have an ulterior motive, but it wasn't impure in any way. He just wanted to do right by his faith.

God knows the heart.

He grabbed the rag out of the back pocket of his jeans then wiped the sweat from his forehead. "You don't care much about my actions if my heart ain't right, do You, Lord?" He shoved the rag back in his pocket. "The world has plenty of do-gooders, but this is about me and You."

Drew pushed away from the dump truck. He walked to the oversized blue cooler he'd been using for water bottles. He opened the lid and grabbed one out. After shutting the lid, he plopped onto the top of the cooler. Resting his elbows and forearms on the tops of his legs, he ducked his head. "God, You know I'm awful prideful. Sometimes it works good—when it comes to farming or building things or odd jobs. I always do a good job. But sometimes that pride makes me not such a nice person."

He lifted his gaze up to the heavens. The summer sky was a beautiful clear blue with just a smattering of cotton candy–like clouds. The midday sun was hot, and he twisted off the cap to the water then took a long swig. He ducked his head again.

"Something about Melody really rubs me wrong, and I'm not myself when I'm around her. I don't like who I am, and I know You don't either. Forgive me again, God. Show me how to be a witness to that woman."

He stood and stretched his back. The long hours keeping up the farm and working on his new home had stretched, pulled, and stiffened his muscles, especially in his back. He made his way back to the dump truck and checked the oil once more and the starter. Everything looked good.

Knowing she should be ready for business, he hopped into the cab and turned the ignition. Nothing. Not even a whine or a groan.

He turned the key and pulled it out of the ignition. Shoving it back into place, he twisted again. Still no sound. *You've got to be kidding me.*

He hopped out of the cab and looked at the engine again. The spark plugs looked good, as did the engine, the starter—everything. It all looked to be in good working order.

Jumping back in the cab, he tried to start her one more time. Still no sound. *I cannot believe this.*

Drew stomped back to his pickup. He fumed as he drove toward town. His cell phone buzzed, and he pulled it out of his front pocket. Seeing Mike's name on the screen, he pushed the TALK button. "Mike, I need your help."

"Okay. I need a favor as well, but go ahead. What's going on?"

"The dump truck won't start."

"I thought Melody was going to take a look at it."

Drew clenched his teeth so tight he felt his jaw would break. He gripped the steering wheel. "She did come by, but she left."

"What did you do?" Mike's tone flattened.

"I didn't do anything. She came out here and looked at it." Drew spit out the words. He could feel his blood pressure rising. He had to get that dump truck working so he could finish leveling off the site to get the foundation going. He didn't have time to play games with some crazy, two-bit woman.

Mike spoke again. "She couldn't fix it?"

"She *wouldn't* fix it. The woman thought I brought her out here to charm her or something."

Mike's guttural laugh sounded over the line. "You? Make a move on her?"

His friend's words struck a nerve, and Drew suddenly felt the urge to grab hold of Mike and punch him a good one. It wouldn't be such an amazing feat for Drew to find the woman attractive. Melody was a very pretty girl, and when she wasn't around Drew, she seemed to be fairly nice.

He knew they had their no-woman pact and all, but it was obvious Wyatt and Nick didn't care much about it. Maybe he didn't care so much anymore either.

Drew shook his head. What was he thinking? He wasn't about to even consider that spitfire in any kind of romantic notion. The idea was preposterous. He barked at Mike, "Will you help me or not?"

"You know I'll help you, but I know—by far—less about vehicles than you do."

"I know." Drew clicked the phone off and focused on the road. He really was trying to catch the wind asking Mike for mechanical help. If Nick were back from his honeymoon, the two of them together could probably figure it out, but Nick wouldn't be back for well over another week. Drew wanted to be working on the foundation by then.

If that woman hadn't gone and gotten all hoity-toity, she could have fixed the truck, and I would have been leveling the ground right now. Admitting he needed her help tasted as bitter as battery acid, and he didn't like it. Not one bit.

four

Drew had given up. He'd worked on the dump truck for a week with no success. Mike looked at it, even though Drew knew that wouldn't do any good. Drew's dad looked at, as did Nick's dad, Roy, and another one of the town's mechanics. Drew could have whooped his own tail when Roy figured out it was the ignition. After he and Roy fixed it, the rotten truck still wouldn't run. Obviously, Roy had been wrong.

He tossed the wrench he was holding to the ground. It was ridiculous that the truck wouldn't run. From the eye of a mechanic, it had every reason to work. He'd borrowed and rented the heavy machinery he needed, and he was on a tight schedule with some of the equipment. He bit back a growl. *I can't get started on the foundation if I can't finish leveling out the ground.*

He wiped sweat from his brow. It was still early June, but Drew knew the summer months would pass him by all too soon. Though not in a big hurry for completion, he'd still hoped to have the house built by fall, the electric and plumbing all ready before winter, and to be living in his new house by Christmas. *At this rate, I'll have to spend another year living with my parents.*

At twenty-six and with two of his best buddies already married off and his baby sister married to one of them, Drew was beginning to feel like quite a moocher still living in his parents' house. He had no plans of landing himself a wife, but he sure needed to feel like he was his own man. Not sleeping under his daddy's roof.

He growled as he walked toward what should have already been leveled land. He folded his arms across his chest and stared out at the pond. He'd spent many a night dreaming of sitting on his own back deck and watching the moon bathe the water with light.

His last option in getting the truck working again was to call Melody. The idea churned his stomach. He'd heard she'd taken a job at AJ's Auto Shop and that everyone in town was singing her praises when it came to her mechanic abilities. There were people coming from their neighboring towns with their trucks and tractors to see if the "pretty little woman," as many of the old-timers called her, could fix their vehicles as good as they'd heard. So far, she seemed to have surpassed everyone's expectations.

Drew shook his head. The notion of that little gal digging around and under those oversized vehicles just didn't seem right. She was too arrogant, too small, even a little too pretty to be doing a job like that. She should be tending the garden or cooking. . . . Drew let out a huff. The woman could fix a truck, but he would bet his best head of cattle that she couldn't cook a decent meal if she tried.

What do I care if the woman has a way with mechanics or if she can or can't cook? Again, he thought of Wyatt's scolding that Drew was too competitive. *And why would I feel so threatened by the woman?*

He picked up a small stone, walked closer to the pond, then threw it, watching as it skipped along the top of the water. All these thoughts weren't getting him anywhere.

He needed to find someone to fix the dump truck, and he didn't care if he was being silly—he had no intention of asking Melody Markwell for help. Instead, he'd just have to pay extra to have someone drive down from Lexington or Louisville.

He turned and headed toward his pickup. He'd have to go home and call around to find out who he needed to get to look at it. The sound of gravel crunching beneath tires drew his attention to the road. He smiled and waved when he realized it was his dad. Then he saw who was in the passenger seat.

He groaned and squinted to the heavens. *Lord, help me to be nice. I can't stand that woman.*

His dad stopped the truck then stepped out of the cab. He patted Drew's shoulder a bit too hard. He understood his dad meant for him to be nice. If he could say it out loud, he'd assure his dad that though a war of fury was raging inside him that his dad would go behind his back like that, Drew would make every attempt to be a gentleman to the much-too-cocky and snappy gal. His dad cleared his throat. "Brought you some help for the dump truck."

"I see that." Drew tried to smile as he spit the words through clenched teeth. Everything in him wanted to tell her to go home. He couldn't believe she'd thought he'd bring her out here for sinister motives. Not only did it go against everything he believed as a Christian, but it also hurt his pride that she would think him that kind of guy.

Melody hopped out of the cab then grabbed her toolbox from the bed of the truck. She walked toward Drew. "I'm doing this for your father, and only because he agreed not to sell his 1967 Mustang until I've had the chance to save enough money to buy it."

Drew gasped. He looked at his dad. "Your Mustang? What? Dad, what is she talking about?"

His dad waved his hand in front of his face. "I was planning on selling her in a few months. Melody's taken quite a liking to her, and I knew she'd be in good hands if Melody bought her off me."

Melody headed to the dump truck. Drew stared at his dad. "Since when were you going to sell the Mustang?"

He nodded to the woman who now had the upper half of her body stuck underneath the steering wheel of the truck. "Since I saw that little lady's eyes light up the first time she saw it."

"But you love that car."

His dad looked at him. "Really? You think so. I bought that thing three years ago, and I still haven't taken the time to get her running. Melody'd have her on the road in a week's time."

"But you don't just sell your car because—"

"No buts. I want to do it." His dad crossed his arms in front of his chest and leaned against his pickup. He nodded toward Melody. "That woman's a good girl. God wants her. She's had a hard life, and she hasn't decided yet if she trusts Him. In every way I can, I want to show her that she can."

Drew watched as Melody worked on the truck. His dad's words stung, and he had a feeling his dad intended for them to. He walked to Melody and cleared his throat. "Do you need any help?"

"Nope." Her tone sounded tense, but he wasn't sure if it was from concentration on the truck or frustration with him. He figured it was probably a little of both.

"I appreciate you doing this." He tried to sound kind and sincere. At the moment, he felt more like a scolded little pup.

"No problem."

He heard a popping noise, and then she lifted herself out of the truck and swiped her hands along her hips. "All done. She should work for you now."

"Are you kidding?" Drew looked at his watch. "That fast?"

She pointed toward the ignition. "Try her out."

He hopped into the truck and turned the key. The oversized machine roared to life. He turned it off then started it again to ensure it wasn't a fluke. Sure enough, it started up again. "I can't believe it."

He studied the ignition. He couldn't tell what she'd done, and he couldn't bring himself to ask her either.

Melody picked up her toolbox and walked back toward his dad's pickup. Drew jumped out of the dump truck and grabbed her arm from behind. On what seemed to be a reflex, she jerked around with her fist clenched. He let her go but stared into her well-guarded eyes. "I just wanted to thank you."

She relaxed a bit and nodded her head. "You're welcome."

Drew watched as she got into the truck beside his dad. She'd jumped like she was terrified of him. He'd never seen a woman so ready to fight at such a simple touch. She had a reason to fear being alone with a man. He saw it for the briefest moment in her eyes. His heart pounded, and anger flamed within him as he thought of what could have happened to her. He'd never allow a woman to be mistreated.

❧

Melody hated Sundays. She'd been living with her aunt and uncle for several months, and the first few months she'd been able to talk her way out of going to church services with them. But the last three months, between Aunt Renee and Uncle Roy, and Gracie's and Addy's constant prodding, Melody had to succumb to their requests or listen to them harp at her for the rest of the week.

She wiped her sweaty palms against the sides of her faded blue jeans as they walked into the pristine white building. They may have been able to get her to go with them, but she absolutely refused to get dressed up. It had been hard enough wearing that silver silky thing in Addy and Nick's wedding. There was no way she'd be dolling herself up for a place she didn't even want to go.

"How ya doin', Melody?" The plump and short, balding pastor grabbed her hand in a tight squeeze.

She nodded and plastered a smile to her face. "I'm fine. Thanks."

He patted the top of her hand. "It always makes my day to see your pretty face come through those doors."

Normally, Melody would deck a man for saying something like that to her, but the pastor's expression and tone was so genuine and sweet, Melody had never been able to allow herself to get mad at him. "It's good to be here."

The words slipped from her mouth, even though she knew they were a lie. It wasn't good to be there. Not to her. She hated sitting in that padded wooden pew beside her aunt and uncle and looking at the wooden cross the church people had hung above a pool of water. If she remembered right, her aunt had said it was a baptistery, whatever that meant.

She felt like such a hypocrite going to church. She didn't believe in God. Well, maybe she believed in Him, but she didn't think He was like this all-present, all-knowing, all-caring being like her family did. He certainly hadn't been very present in her life.

If He was all the terrific things her aunt and uncle talked about, then why did He let her dad leave? Why did her mom work all the time and ignore her when she was home? Why did that guy try to rape her? Why did her mom up and decide to get married again?

Those were only the whys about her own life. She had a plethora of whys when it came to the really bad things that happened in the world. The people who were abused by their parents. The people who were murdered. Car accidents. Drug abuse. Drunk drivers. Hurricanes. Tornadoes. The list literally went on and on and on.

If God was in control of all the world—the whole wide world—and He loved the world so much that He gave His only Son, as her aunt liked to remind her, then Melody wanted to know why He allowed so many bad things to happen.

She shook her head. No. Either there wasn't a God, or He just liked to keep Himself out of all the happenings of the world. Whichever of the two was true of God, she wanted nothing to do with Him.

The only being who could control her life was Melody. She had been the one who tried to fight off the man who attacked her. She had been the one who helped her mom in every way possible while growing up. She was the one who got herself through diesel mechanic school and then worked hard to be one of the best at it. She was the one in control, and she didn't need to attend some feel-good church service to make her think all the things she couldn't explain would be all right in the end.

"Hi, Melody."

Melody turned at the sound of her name. She smiled at one of the older ladies in the church. Sweet, tiny Bonnie suffered from rheumatoid arthritis. Over the years, her hands had gnarled until she had almost no use of her individual fingers. Melody knew the woman had to be in pain most of, if not all, the time. Yet Bonnie always wore a smile on her face. She even painted wooden ornaments her husband cut for her. The woman was a true encouragement in never giving up, and her sweet spirit drew Melody.

"Hi, Bonnie." Melody reached toward the woman and wrapped her arms around her. Bonnie felt more like a grandmother to her than a church acquaintance, and she made sitting through church every week worth it.

"I made these for all the ladies. I got them done a little early, but"—Bonnie held up a small flag pin—"they're to wear on the Fourth of July."

Melody took the wooden pin painted in red, white, and blue. "Thank you so much."

Bonnie waved. "Church is getting ready to start. You have a good day."

Melody stared at the pin as Bonnie walked to the other side of the sanctuary. *Why would God allow that kind woman to live in constant pain?*

Why is that woman so kind?

Melody blinked at the second thought. She had no idea where it had come from. She wasn't sure what to think about it either. Her brows furrowed as she lowered herself into her seat. She felt her aunt and uncle beside her, and she nodded to Gracie and Wyatt from across the aisle, but she felt perplexed by the thought.

What did make Bonnie different?

She looked at her aunt and uncle. The music leader instructed the congregation to stand as the first song of the morning began. She never actually sang the words but mouthed along with everyone instead. She studied her aunt's and uncle's faces. She knew there was something different about them. Even when she was a girl, she could tell they had a peace, a joy that she didn't understand.

Oh, she'd seen them fuss before. She remembered one time when she was a little girl and Uncle Roy hadn't started the grill when Aunt Renee thought he had. She and her mom had all the food ready, and not only was the grill not hot, but it was out of propane as well. Aunt Renee was not happy, and she made sure her husband knew it. But even then, the way they handled their fight, they were different.

The music finally ended, and Melody sat and prepared herself to listen to their preacher for forty-five minutes or so. Today one of the women walked to the podium and picked up the microphone. Music started, and she began to sing. She had the most beautiful, soothing voice, and Melody was instantly drawn into the song. Something about being able to call down angels to destroy everything, but instead Jesus had died for all of us.

The song ended, and Aunt Renee leaned over and swiped moisture from her eye. "I love that song, and no one sings it like Tammie."

Melody nodded but continued to stare at the front of the church. This time the preacher did walk to the podium. Most of the time, she tried to envision the engine of whatever vehicle she needed to work on. Today, he talked about storms of life and how we wouldn't know the answers to all our questions this side of heaven. "Some things we just won't understand," the pastor's voice boomed through the sanctuary.

Why not, God? Why won't You tell us?

She inwardly chided herself for talking to a being that she wasn't completely convinced existed. She looked around her at all the people she'd met over the last few months. Spying Drew and his parents on her right, she studied him. He'd been on her like grease on a muffler practically since the day she'd moved to River Run. He didn't like her mechanical know-how one bit. It was obvious he was threatened by her. But he was supposed to be a Christian as well.

She thought about him thanking her when she fixed his dump truck and about how offended he'd looked when she'd accused him of taking her to his homesite alone for wrong reasons. He was gruff and grumpy, but if she were honest, he'd never been cruel to her.

"Let me close with what Jesus told us in John 16:33." The pastor's voice interrupted her thoughts, and she turned her attention back to him. "God's Word says, 'I have told you these things, so that in me you may have peace. In this world you will have trouble. But take heart! I have overcome the world.'"

Melody bowed her head as the pastor led the congregation in prayer. Her mind whirled with everything she'd heard this morning. It was more than she wanted to think about. In fact, a slight headache had started to pulse above her left eye.

So God warned them they'd have trouble. Told everyone

it was part of life on earth. But that didn't explain why. She needed to understand why. The pulse above her eye quickened. Actually, she needed a nap.

Once the service had been dismissed, her body tightened when Drew started to walk toward them. He extended his hand to her. Knowing she couldn't be rude in front of everyone, she shook his hand. He was so much bigger and stronger than she. Something about that made her feel uncomfortable and protected at the same time.

Lifting her chin to force the vulnerable feelings that washed over her to pass through, she peered into his cool eyes. Sincerity and warmth shown from their depths, and Melody found herself swallowing a knot that had formed in her throat.

"I wanted to thank you again for fixing the truck."

He held her hand a bit too long, and Melody felt a thrill at the coarseness of his palm—proof that he was a man who didn't shy away from hard work. She pulled her hand away and tried not to flinch as his kind gaze became almost more than she could bear. "Again, you're welcome."

Today of all days, she did not need to endure the kind side of Drew Wilson. She wanted the man to be normal with her, to fuss and fight with her, to do something that was not so attractive.

She gasped at the thought. The last thing she would think of Drew was that he was attractive. Sick with herself for the thought, she wiped her hand on her jeans and wrinkled her nose.

Drew's expression changed. He must have thought she meant she was disgusted to have touched his hand. Fury swept across his face. A smile tickled the side of her mouth as she knew he was about to light into her. *Now that's the Drew I need to see.*

Lifting one eyebrow, she cocked her head. "Something wrong, Drew?"

"Not a thing." Drew whipped around and walked out of the sanctuary.

To his credit, he didn't fuss at her within the church's walls, but she knew he wanted to. She smirked. *A good Christian wouldn't get so bent out of shape so fast.*

As she walked down the aisle to the door, she tried not think about the fact that Drew hadn't given in to his anger but had walked out the door before saying an unkind word.

five

Melody woke up with a start. She flung off the covers and sat up, wiping the sweat from her forehead. Twisting her body, she allowed her legs to fall off the side of the bed. She placed her elbows on her knees and cupped her cheeks with her hands. She took long, slow breaths, in and out, in and out.

The nightmare had returned. This was the third time in only one week she'd awakened this way. It didn't make sense why they would happen now. It had been over ten years since that day. She thought she'd gotten over it—put it in the back of her mind forever. And yet here it was—like the cobra being charmed out of its basket by the sound of the flutelike instrument— the nightmare had returned.

She could still smell his stale cigarette breath, still feel his firm, strong grasp. She'd never felt so alone, so scared, so vulnerable. Though she'd tried to fight him, in less than a moment, the man had complete control of her. He'd pushed her down in the bushes. When she remembered like this, she could still feel the small twigs break beneath her weight and the stronger ones claw at her back.

Just above her tailbone, she'd hit a root from a tree that towered just a few feet away. The deep bruise it made stayed with her in color and in pain for nearly a month. When she tried to scream, he'd cupped her mouth with one hand and blew into her face trying to shush her. His breath had parted her bangs, and droplets of his spit smacked her eyes.

Fear she'd never known gripped her as she realized with each breath that he had more and more control of her. *How could this be happening? This isn't happening*, raced through her mind time and again.

Then as quickly as he'd attacked her, he was gone. A blond-haired woman with a little baby in a stroller in front of her reached her hand down to Melody. She held some kind of black device in her other hand. It looked like a container of mace.

"Let me help you," the woman said as she brushed leaves and twigs out of Melody's face. Panic, embarrassment, and fear wrapped themselves around her again, and Melody pushed the woman away and raced back to her house. She'd locked the door and shoved a chair beneath the doorknob until her mother got home.

Blowing the memories out with a long breath, she padded out of the bedroom and into the bathroom. She turned on lukewarm water and washed her face. Opening her eyes, she stared at her reflection in the mirror. She looked tired. She *was* tired.

She didn't want this nightmare to come back. Though she had begrudged the money she spent on it, Melody was able to convince her mother to enroll her in a self-defense class after that day. Melody knew how to defend herself. She knew when and how to fight and get away. If anyone ever caught her off guard again, she was prepared. *Of course, I'll never allow myself to be caught off guard again.*

Thankful that it was morning, even if it was a bit earlier than she'd intended to wake up and the sun had not yet made its appearance, Melody brushed her teeth and her hair then slipped on a pair of shorts and a T-shirt. Not ready for breakfast, she walked outside to Aunt Renee's garden.

The small plants had grown so much. She knelt beside the cucumbers, her designated row, and pulled weeds that had started to grow around them. She and her aunt had to be consistent in plucking the weeds out of the garden. The vegetables wouldn't be able to grow if the unwanted foliage overtook them.

She wanted the nightmare out of her mind, but while plucking the weeds, she began to wonder if she would always deal with that particular mental weed—if she would continuously have to fight the fear of what could have happened.

Sometimes she didn't feel strong enough. She'd never admit that aloud. Everyone believed she was strong enough for anything, and she wanted them to believe that. But there were times, like this morning, that she wanted nothing more than to succumb to the fear she felt.

"You're out bright and early."

Melody jumped at the sound of Aunt Renee's voice behind her. She turned and stood, forcing a smile to her face. "Yep. I woke up early."

Her aunt waved her hand across the garden. "Looks like you've been busy."

Melody looked down. She had weeded a lot more than she'd realized. She must have been deep in thought. She chuckled. "I suppose I have."

"You wanna make some pancakes before the girls come to get you?"

Melody sucked in her breath and covered her mouth with her hand. "I completely forgot."

"How could you forget a shopping trip?" Her aunt winked and wrapped her arm around Melody's shoulders as she guided her toward the back door. "They're coming at eight, right?"

"Yeah." Melody looked heavenward, realizing the sun had already risen. *How could I have possibly missed a sunrise? I must be losing my mind.* "What time is it?"

"It's a little after seven." Aunt Renee opened the back door and guided her inside. "Why don't I make the pancakes while you go get cleaned up?"

Melody stopped, placed her hand on her hip, and grinned at her aunt. "Are you suggesting I don't look good enough for a shopping trip?"

"Not suggesting, honey. I'm telling you straight-out."

Melody laughed as she made her way to the hall bathroom again.

"Maybe keep your hair down today. It's so beautiful," her aunt's voice sounded from the kitchen.

Melody didn't respond. She almost never wore her hair down in public. She didn't want to look girlish or vulnerable, as she sometimes felt. After a quick shower, she put on fresh clothes and brushed and blow-dried her long, dark hair. It was pretty. Thick and wavy, heavy as it could possibly be. Taking a deep breath, she decided she'd let it fall down her back as her aunt suggested.

She opened the drawer to put her brush away and spied the mascara she'd used for Addy's wedding. A little brightening of the eyes might not hurt either. After all, she was going shopping with friends. Before she could change her mind, she swiped on a coat of the black stuff and then surveyed her reflection. She looked a lot more feminine, but she still felt like herself. A part of her actually enjoyed it.

Wonder what Drew would think. . . .

Ugh. She wanted to knot her hair into the tightest bun possible and scrub the mascara from her eyes at the thought. She refused to care what Drew Wilson thought about her appearance. The man drove her crazy.

She walked out of the bathroom and back to the kitchen.

"Well, lookie here!" Uncle Roy jumped up from his seat and hugged Melody. He placed a soft kiss on the top of her head. "Prettiest girl I've seen in a long time."

Aunt Renee wiped her hands on a dish towel. She walked to Melody and pushed a long strand of hair over her shoulder. "Honey, you are absolutely beautiful. And such a natural beauty, too."

Melody's cheeks warmed at her aunt and uncle's praise. She rarely received compliments about her appearance. They usually came in the form of her mechanical abilities. She couldn't deny their words felt nice.

"Thank you." Trying to change the topic, she pointed to the pancakes on the table. "These mine?"

Her aunt nodded, and Melody slid into the chair and swallowed down two pancakes before she heard Gracie pull into the driveway. She hopped up and placed her plate in the sink. "Thanks, Aunt Renee."

"You have fun."

Her aunt's words sounded from behind as she raced out the door. Gracie's whistle pealed through the air when Melody stepped off the front porch. "Look at you!" she squealed.

Melody's face warmed as she walked to the car and slipped inside. "I don't look *that* different."

"Oh yes you do, and this settles it." She flipped a strand of Melody's hair. "We're going to find you a cute outfit or two while we're out. You're entirely too pretty to wear coveralls, faded blue jeans, and old T-shirts all the time."

Melody rolled her eyes. "Just go pick up Addy and her friend. What's the girl's name?"

"Val. She and Addy were roommates in college. You'll love her."

Melody nodded and stared out the window. This morning she'd had the nightmare that had terrorized her too many times already in her life. Now she was going shopping with a group of girls who wanted to transform her into a pretty woman. It seemed the most ridiculous thing she could do, and yet she wanted to change. She wanted to feel different. Maybe a change in the way she looked would do the trick and help her put the past behind her.

When they pulled into Addy and Nick's driveway, Melody jumped out of the car and raced to the front porch to give Addy a hug. She hadn't seen her friend since her wedding. Taking in Addy's beautiful, long, blond hair and glowing green eyes, Melody smirked at her. "Someone sure looks happy."

Addy bit her bottom lip and giggled. "Being married is a lot of fun."

The tall, thin woman with bright red hair clipped in the shortest, spikiest hairstyle Melody had ever seen extended her hand. "You must be Melody. I'm Val, Addy's roommate from college."

Addy moved her eyebrows up and down. "I hear we're doing a bit of a makeover on someone today."

Melody giggled, a sound she never thought would come

from her own lips. "Believe it or not, I'm going to let you."

Addy clapped her hands then brushed her fingers through Melody's hair. She looked at her friend, Val. "With her dark hair and eyes, she'd be beautiful in yellow. Don't you think, Val? I've always wanted to wear yellow, but I'm too fair."

"Oh, and soft pink. She'll look gorgeous," Val added.

Melody felt dizzy as they led her to Gracie's car. "What were we going shopping for to begin with?" she asked as the three women continued to talk about the colors Melody should wear.

"Sweetie, we were going to try to make you over all along." Gracie smacked the top of the steering wheel. "We thought it would be a battle, but you're already willing. Wonders never cease."

"Amen, sister." Addy lifted her hand for Gracie to give her a high five.

"God is always working, even with the small stuff," Val added.

Melody's body stiffened. It was always about God with these people in River Run. Even with Addy's friend it was about God. She didn't need God, and He definitely wasn't involved in the small stuff.

She closed her eyes. She wouldn't let the little comments ruin her day. She needed a change—something to get her mind off her past. She'd enjoy acting like a girl. For today anyway.

☙

As they did at least once a month, Drew's parents invited Roy and Renee, Nick and Addy, and Melody to their house for a cookout. He'd felt anxious about seeing Melody again. She'd seemed pressed on his heart all week. The girl needed

Jesus. It was as obvious as a car's need for gas. Today, Drew was determined to keep the peace with the woman and be a good witness to her.

Roy and Renee pulled into the driveway. Drew could hardly believe his eyes when Melody stepped out of the car. She didn't even look like herself. Her hair cascaded like a waterfall almost all the way to her stomach on one side. Even from a distance, he could see long dark eyelashes framing chocolate-colored eyes. She wore a light pink sundress and carried a small purse in her left hand. Even at the wedding, she hadn't carried any kind of purse.

The woman was a vision. He hadn't been able to get her out of his mind since Sunday, having felt her inner struggle with God. Now, he'd never be able to get how beautiful she was out of his head either.

"Do you need some help carrying anything?" Drew hollered to Renee.

"Come get the deviled eggs," she called back.

Drew nodded to Melody as he walked past her to the car. She held a dessert in one hand, probably Renee's homemade blackberry cobbler, and a bowl of coleslaw in the other. He grabbed the eggs from the car and shut the door.

Roy nudged Drew with his elbow. "She's awful pretty all dolled up like that, ain't she?"

Drew lifted his eyebrows. "She sure is."

He followed Roy into the house and placed the eggs on the table. Sitting beside his new brother-in-law, Nick, in the great room, he tried to watch the baseball game on television, but his gaze kept wandering to the women gathered around the kitchen counters.

He believed Melody even had a shade of pink lipstick or

lip gloss or whatever it was called on her lips. He noticed how full they were. Though he'd inwardly criticized them at the wedding, he could tell they were just the perfect shape and size for a kiss.

He wrinkled his nose at the thought as Nick's elbow landed hard into his ribs. He frowned at his lifelong friend. "What was that for?"

Nick raised his eyebrows and nodded toward the women. "You gonna be next to fall? Mike gonna win the bet?"

Drew huffed. "I thought the bet was off."

Nick shrugged. "Technically, it is. Addy would string me by my neck if she thought it wasn't." He twisted until he could stare full into Drew's face. "I'm just wondering if you're gonna be next to fall."

Drew shifted on the couch as he lifted his left foot to his right knee. He brushed the hem of his blue jeans with his hand. "I don't know why you'd think that."

"'Cause you got a thing for my cousin."

Drew whispered to his friend, "First of all, I don't have a thing for your cousin. Second of all, your cousin is fighting God something fierce. She's not even an option for me to have a thing for."

Nick's expression sobered. "I know. My family keeps praying for her. She's going to church with them every week, and God's Word never comes back void." He sighed. "But it's still her decision to accept Him, and so far she hasn't."

The women laughed, and Drew turned his attention back to them. He felt an urgency for Melody to accept Christ into her life. Seeing her dressed as a woman, noting how tiny she truly was, Drew felt an overwhelming need to protect her from all harm. He realized he truly cared about her.

"All right, guys"—Drew's mother waved at the men—"come get your plates."

Drew loaded his plate with the best straight-from-scratch foods in River Run. Coleslaw and potato salad; baked beans and deviled eggs; pickled beets and sweet tea. Even the hamburgers came from one of his dad's best Anguses. He spied Renee's blackberry cobbler over on the kitchen counter, and his mouth already salivated at the thought of biting into the dessert.

If it weren't for the fact that he, his dad, Nick, and Roy all had to work hard on their family farms, all four of them would be big as barns from the good cooking these women whipped up. Roy actually had put on a few pounds since he'd had to retire early, but the Wii game Renee bought him had helped him keep the weight under control.

After saying grace, Drew scooped up a forkful of coleslaw and shoveled it into his mouth. Surprised by the sour taste, he gagged and spit the food back onto his plate. He covered his mouth and looked at the peering eyes of his family and friends around the table. His face warmed, as he knew his mother would reprimand him for being so rude. But he hadn't meant to. He loved Renee's coleslaw. If he was unsure about the taste of a dish, he'd take a small bite first. But he knew hers was the best in the county, and he'd scooped the mouthful in. With the bitter taste—well, it just popped right out.

"Drew!" His mother's voice sounded tense.

"I'm sorry. I got too big of a bite." He averted his gaze from Renee. He didn't want her to think he didn't like her cooking.

"It's okay, Drew," Renee said. He looked at her as she took a small bite of the coleslaw. Her face scrunched up as if she'd just bitten into a lemon. She wiped her mouth. "It's not your fault. I must have forgotten the sugar."

"*You* didn't forget the sugar." Melody growled as her face flamed the brightest red Drew had ever seen. "*I* forgot the sugar." She smacked her napkin on the table, and tears welled in her eyes as she stared at Addy, Renee, and his mom. "I'm never going to be like you." She pushed away from the table and walked down the hall and into the bathroom.

"I'm sorry." Drew felt like a complete and total heel. Melody must have made the coleslaw and forgot a main ingredient. He glanced at Renee. "You know I love your coleslaw. I just took a big ol' bite, and when it hit my tongue, it just came right back out."

Roy lifted his hand. "It's all right, Drew. You didn't aim to hurt Melody's feelings."

Renee added, "Let's just not make a big deal about this. It's best we just go ahead and act normal. She'll feel better when she comes out if we're all acting normal."

Drew tried to eat the rest of his food. It all tasted the same—bland. He didn't overly like Melody, but he didn't want to hurt her feelings or embarrass her, either. She never came out of the bathroom. He could hear Addy trying to talk to her, and he considered trying to go back to the bathroom and apologize, but he was afraid it would make her more upset. With a sigh of frustration, he decided he should go outside with the other men.

They started a game of cornhole. Drew and his dad against Roy and Nick. It would be an easy game, as it always was. He and his dad could whip up on Roy and Nick even if they gave them a five-point lead from the beginning.

Drew turned when the back screen door smacked against the doorjamb. Addy and Melody walked toward two foldable chairs under the oversized oak tree. Melody had pulled her hair back in a ponytail, and Drew could tell she'd cleaned the makeup off her face. She still looked pretty, and Drew wished he could think of a way to apologize to her about the coleslaw.

"Drew, you entering the tractor pull?" Roy asked.

Drew scoffed as he looked back at the men. "You know I am. There ain't nobody got a tractor as sweet as mine." Drew gawked at Nick. "You gonna try to take me on this Fourth of July?"

Nick chortled and took a few steps back. "Oh no. Now that I'm hitched, I haven't had time to work on souping up a tractor."

"Excuse me, Nick Martin?" Drew turned toward his sister and Melody. Addy had her hands on her hips. "Are you begrudging being hitched?"

Nick raced to his new wife, wrapped his arms around her, lifted her off the ground, and spun her around. "Not in the slightest. I love my little ball and chain."

"Nick Martin!" Addy teasingly swatted his shoulders until Nick planted a long kiss on her lips.

Disgusted and yet feeling the oddest nudging of jealousy, Drew rolled his eyes and looked back at Roy. "Guess the only competition I've ever had won't be showing up."

"I'll be there." Melody walked toward them, her arms crossed in front of her chest.

"What?" Drew frowned.

"I'll be competing in the tractor pull."

Drew laughed.

"I'm serious."

Drew widened his stance and placed his hands on his hips. He let out a long breath. "I'm sure you are serious, but you have no business competing in the tractor pull."

"Why?" She cocked her head and squinted at him. "Because I'm a just a little, wimpy woman?"

There she went with the "little, wimpy" comments again. He had never suggested she was wimpy; however, she was little—tiny in height and frame.

Drew spread his arms out. "Why do you have to be so competitive? Why do you have to prove yourself all the time?"

"Why do you have to be the best of everything all the time? Why can't you lose?"

Drew ground his teeth. He intertwined his fingers and lifted his hands to his lips. Inwardly, he counted to ten, willing himself not to explode and say something to her that he'd later regret. He swallowed and nodded his head. "Okay, Melody. I'll see you there."

He turned and stomped toward the house. He'd had about all he could take of Melody Markwell. Girl or no girl, at that tractor pull he was going to knock that little spitfire off her high horse.

six

Drew checked the Continental AV1790 tank engine he'd put in the tractor. He liked this particular one because it was an American engine used to pilot heavy tanks. He hopped onto the seat of the tractor and started her up. She roared to life, just as he expected.

He smiled at the power he could feel beneath him. He wouldn't have any trouble pulling the sled. It wouldn't matter that the weights pushed forward on the sled's axles, making the front of it push into the ground. His engine would rip right through the dirt and keep pulling at a good, strong pace the full one hundred meters.

Everyone he knew came out for the annual Independence Day event that took place in the town's fairgrounds. The fact that the town allowed vending stands to start setting up last year made the tractor pull quite an event. They'd sell funnel cakes and popcorn, hot dogs and hamburgers. He'd heard someone was setting up a blooming onion stand. His mouth watered at the thought of the fried vegetable dipped in that delicious pinkish-colored sauce. After winning, he'd be sure to get him one of those.

Once the truck and tractor pull finished and it started to get dark, the sheriff's department would set off fireworks. For a small town, Drew had been impressed by the good show they'd been able to put on, but then the sheriff's son-in-law had a brother in Tennessee who sold them fireworks at a discounted rate.

In the back of his mind, he still wondered about Melody's tractor and engine. He'd learned the hard way he couldn't take that gal for granted. She was a talented mechanic; he couldn't deny it. But if she had to work with what Nick and Roy had to offer with their tractor, then Drew shouldn't have any trouble showing her who was the boss of the tractor pull.

He turned off the tractor and jumped down. He'd planned to work on finishing up the foundation of his house today, but he had to make sure the tractor was ready first. The tractor pull was in a little over a week, and he'd never be able to show his face in town again if Melody beat him.

He spotted Mike's truck driving along the dirt road leading to the barn. He waved at his friend, and Mike parked and stuck his arm out the window. "Whatcha doin?"

Drew patted the tractor. "Getting ready for the pull. Did you hear Melody's planning to race?"

"I heard." Mike patted the side of the truck. "The woman's just itching to prove herself."

"She sure is."

"Sounds like someone else I know."

Drew squinted at Mike. "Now, what's that supposed to mean?"

"Not supposed to mean anything." He motioned for Drew to get in the truck. "Come on. It's lunchtime, and I'm heading to the diner."

Drew's stomach growled when Mike mentioned food. He hadn't realized it had gotten so late. Noting the sun high in the sky, he realized he'd been out working on the tractor longer than he thought. If he didn't watch it, he was going to get behind on his farmwork. "Sounds good. Take me by the house to clean up a bit."

He got in the truck, and Mike drove to the house. Drew hurried into the bathroom and washed his face and hands and changed his shirt. Most everyone went to the diner just as they were after a hard morning's work on the farm, but Drew's mom would have his hide if he didn't at least clean up enough that he wasn't covered in dirt and smell of cows and sweat. After running a brush through his hair, he went back outside and got in the truck with Mike.

As they headed to the diner, Drew's thoughts jumbled with all he needed to do for the house and the farm, and yet now he was worried about not having his tractor fixed up enough. When he thought rationally, he knew his competitiveness with Melody was ridiculous. Normally, he'd never even consider going against a girl in a tractor pull.

It was her attitude. He just couldn't get past how the woman thought she needed to beat a man, him in particular, at everything. He bet if he had his mom show him how to stitch a quilt, that fool-brained woman would try to make one that looked better.

He should challenge her to a cooking duel. She'd proven she wasn't any count in the kitchen. Drew sighed at his mean thought. She'd been so embarrassed over the coleslaw, and he'd felt lower than the gum stuck to the bottom of a shoe that he'd been the one to inadvertently call her out on it. Mike and Wyatt both warned him that he and Melody were a lot alike when it came to their competitive nature. When Drew was honest, he knew it was true.

Mike pulled into a parking space, and the two got out of the truck and headed inside. Drew watched as Lacy's eyes widened when Mike walked toward her. She smiled and blushed when she led them to their usual booth.

Drew shook his head at Mike as the man tried to act as if Lacy's obvious attraction didn't affect him. "I think I may try something different today," Mike said, staring at the menu.

Drew chuckled. "You're not going to try anything different. You're just avoiding eye contact with me, as you do every time we come here and you get a first look at Lacy."

Mike narrowed his eyes. "I am not."

Drew folded his arms on top of the table. "Oh really. What are you going to have different, Mike? You're not going to have meat loaf and mashed potatoes? You and I both know how much you love the meat loaf and mashed potatoes."

"No. I'm not. I'm going to have the Salisbury steak today, or maybe I'll have the country ham." Mike folded the menu and smacked it against the table.

"I don't know why you don't just ask the woman out on a date. You two have been making goo-goo eyes at each other for two years. It's ridiculous. The bet is off. Addy made us call it off."

"Oh really." Mike grabbed the utensils rolled in a paper napkin between his fingers and pointed them at Drew. "So, why don't you go on a date?"

Drew huffed. "There's no one I like."

Mike leaned back against the padded booth. "Really. If you weren't so mule headed, you'd see there is a woman you like. And you like her a lot."

Drew's ire rose, as he knew exactly who his friend was about to say. Wyatt mentioned her, as did Nick, but all three of them seemed to have lost their senses. Melody Markwell was his number-one nemesis, not someone he'd be interested in. "And who would that be?"

Lacy walked up to their booth before Mike could respond, which was lucky for Mike, because Drew planned to kick him hard if he'd said that woman's name. His ire was quickly replaced with humor as he watched his friend swallow hard then look up at Lacy. She averted her gaze from Mike, and Drew grinned as her neck and cheeks blazed bright pink. "What can I get you boys?"

Drew stretched his hands out in front of him. He enjoyed watching the two of them squirm in each other's presence. "Well, Lacy," Drew started, "I think I'm going to try something different today. Give me the country ham and mashed potatoes."

He handed her his menu and grinned when Mike looked up at him and wrinkled his nose and narrowed his eyes.

"What about you, Mike?" Her voice squeaked. "You gonna try something different?"

The woman's tone seemed to plead with him to try something different, as if ordering a Salisbury steak instead of meat loaf would suddenly give him the courage to ask her on a date. He watched as she held her breath. For a moment, Drew felt kind of bad for Lacy. He knew she'd never in a million years ask Mike on a date first. It went against everything they'd all been raised to believe. Course, when he thought about it, he didn't know why it was so wrong for a gal to ask a guy for dinner. It wasn't as if it would *hurt* anything, but still he had to admit he'd rather be the one asking the girl out on the date.

Drew's attention shifted back to his friend and Lacy as

Mike handed the menu to her without looking up. "No. I'll get the usual. Meat loaf and mashed potatoes."

Lacy let out the breath and nodded. "Coming right up." She tucked the menus under her arm and headed back to the kitchen.

Drew burst into laughter as he smacked the table with his hand. "The usual. Really? Mike, I would have never guessed it."

"Laugh at me all you want, Drew. I'm not the only one avoiding women."

Drew laughed again, but this time Mike's words didn't seem so comical. Over the last few weeks, he'd spent more time stewing over what Melody was thinking, doing, or feeling than he had over his farm or the home he was building. It was sobering to think Mike's point was all too true.

❧

Melody lifted Gracie's baby boy out of his high chair. At five months, little Wyatt had grown so much. She wiped the dribbling of rice cereal from his lips with the MOMMY'S LITTLE HELPER bib he wore around his neck. She kissed his fat cheek then cooed at the boy. "Tell your mommy I said thanks so much for inviting me to lunch."

Wyatt Jr. widened his mouth into a full, toothless smile. A cackle escaped as he twisted his body and grabbed at the strands of hair that had fallen out of her ponytail. He was always excited after he'd gotten some food in his belly, and he absolutely adored pulling her long hair.

"We love having you over for lunch," Gracie said as she laid plates of ham sandwiches and baked chips on the table. "Do you want me to take him so you can eat?"

"No. I like holding him."

"But you only have another thirty minutes."

Melody looked at the clock above the table. Her lunch hour always flew by too quickly when she was able to spend it with Gracie and Wyatt Jr.

"That's okay. I can hold him and eat." Melody shoved a bite of sandwich into her mouth. Little Wyatt tried to reach for her mouth as she chewed. She leaned toward him and Eskimo kissed his nose. "It's my turn to eat now, big guy."

Gracie sat across from her and started to talk about her morning. Melody genuinely enjoyed hearing about Wyatt's projectile vomiting and soiled-through diapers. Even though she'd never been a huge fan of men and marriage, she'd always been drawn to children. She hated that she'd probably never have any of her own.

An image of Drew Wilson popped into her head, and she wondered for a moment what his children would look like. She envisioned three rowdy, blond-haired, stair-step boys chasing after a cow. A tiny dark-haired girl fought through the tall grass, running after the boys. She shook her head. Why would she think of that egotistical man? Sometimes the notions her mind conjured up made absolutely no sense.

Gracie continued, "This morning I woke up later than usual, and I didn't have a chance to get my shower before Wyatt woke up. I knew I was going to be miserable for the whole day."

After taking another big bite of sandwich, Melody tickled the baby's chin, and he cackled again. "Was Mommy going to be miserable for you today?"

Gracie tapped the tip of Wyatt's nose, causing him to laugh again, as she went on. "I prayed for God's intervention.

I didn't want to be grumpy just because I woke up late. But then he took a morning nap." Gracie clasped her hands. "I couldn't believe it." She reached over and tickled Wyatt's toes. "This little guy is a wonderful nap taker in the afternoon, but he almost never goes back down in the morning. It was like God's precious gift to me this morning."

Trying to respond in a supportive manner to her friend, Melody raised her eyebrows and nodded. She got so tired of the God-did-this, God-did-that stuff she was inundated with by her family and friends. It was as if these people couldn't take a step without praising or praying to God about it.

She loved her aunt and uncle, and the friends she'd found here were some of the very best she'd ever had. She wouldn't do anything to change them, but she really got tired of it. If Gracie lost her favorite pen, she'd pray about it and say God helped her find it. If she was nervous about taking Wyatt Jr. to the doctor for his shots, she'd pray about it and say God gave her peace. If the sun shone high and the breeze blew perfectly, she'd say praises about how good God was to them. To be honest, Melody was just plain sick of it. The whole wide world didn't revolve around God.

"It doesn't?"

She wanted to growl at the still, small voice that seemed to creep up within her at the weirdest moments. Every time it did, she was forced to think about if she had a few things wrong.

Over the last few weeks, she decided she did believe there was a God—or at least some kind of higher being. The sermons and the comments from her family and friends had made enough sense, and it was true that creation was entirely too intricate and too perfectly put together not to have been formed by something.

So if something did form all of creation—the oceans and mountains, the rivers and valleys, the animals and plants, and the intricate weavings of all those things—would it make sense that the world revolved around it?

Holding the baby with one hand, she rubbed her temple with the other. She'd had more headaches in the last few months than she'd had in her life, and she was still having nightmares. Only now they were about her dad leaving when she was five.

She barely remembered the man, and she definitely had no recollection of him leaving them. He'd gone in the middle of the night, when she was asleep. And yet, for several nights in a row, she'd envisioned him walking out the door and not looking behind him in her dreams.

She'd begun to dread nighttime. She'd grown weary of asking herself why God allowed so many bad things to happen. Now she'd have new questions to invade her thoughts: *Does the world revolve around God? And if the world does revolve around Him, then is Gracie's approach of talking to Him and about Him every day the right way to have a relationship with Him? But again, if the world revolves around God, why does He allow bad things to happen?*

Melody scrunched her nose. It was like a constant circle of unanswered questions. Her brain had never worked this hard before moving to River Run, even when she was learning all she needed to know about mechanics. The pulsing in her temple deepened. "Gracie, do you have any ibuprofen?"

"Sure." Gracie got up and walked to the cabinet. "You have another headache?"

"Yeah."

"Maybe you should see a doctor." Gracie grabbed a water bottle from the refrigerator and handed it to Melody. "You've been looking tired a lot lately."

"I haven't been sleeping well."

Melody placed both pills in her mouth and with one swig of water swallowed them down. Hopefully, they would kick in soon after she got back to AJ's garage. She still had a long day ahead of her with a transmission to fix, and she wanted to look over Uncle Roy's tractor engine one more time. In only a few days, she'd be whipping up on Drew at the fairgrounds.

"I know you may not. . ."

Melody looked up at her friend when she started to talk and then stopped. Gracie bit her bottom lip as if unsure if she should continue. Melody furrowed her eyebrows. "We're friends. You can tell me anything. What's wrong?"

"I was just wondering if you'd let me pray for you."

Melody shrugged. "I don't care. Pray all you want. I'm getting ready to go."

Gracie shook her head. "No. I mean right now. Before you leave. Out loud."

Melody's body stiffened, and she let out a long breath. It was one thing to sit through a church service and bow her head when the pastor told her to or to sit at the dinner table while someone prayed over the food, but to actually have Gracie pray for her—Melody wasn't sure how she felt about that. She gazed over at Gracie, whose expression seemed to plead for Melody to allow her to do it. With a long sigh, Melody nodded. "Okay."

A smile brightened Gracie's face, and before Melody could

protest, she grabbed her hand and squeezed. "Oh dear Jesus, I praise You for my wonderful friend, Melody. I love her so much, Lord. I'm so glad she moved to River Run. Thank You that she comes and eats lunch with Wyatt and me."

Melody had to clear her throat. Tears started to pool in her eyes. Gracie was thankful she came over for lunch? It was the highlight of Melody's day to be able to see them.

Gracie continued, "She's been having headaches, Lord. A lot of them. And she looks tired, God. I don't know what is causing all this, but I pray You will heal Melody. Draw her close to Yourself. Thank You, Jesus. Amen."

Melody had to swallow and blink several times to keep from crying outright in front of Gracie. She handed the baby to his mother and grabbed her coveralls off the chair. After slipping back into the grease-covered garment, she nodded to her friend. "Thanks, Gracie."

Before Gracie could wrap her in a hug, which Melody knew would be coming if she didn't get out of that house fast enough, Melody left. A knife seemed to be stuck in her heart, and it twisted with every step she took. The pulsing in her head grew stronger, and either God wasn't listening or He was saying no to Gracie's request. Either way, Melody was sure of one thing: Gracie had something that she was beginning to realize she wanted. A relationship with God.

seven

Melody rolled onto her back and stretched her arms as far as she could above her head. The sun peeked through the cracks of the closed blinds. Groggy, she gazed at the alarm clock on the nightstand. *Nine o'clock!*

She sat up in a hurry and flung her legs over the bed. *I'm late for work.* The sleep fuzzies in her brain began to clear, and she remembered she didn't have to work today. She smiled just before a yawn took over her mouth.

Hopping off the bed, she padded across the room and peered out her upstairs bedroom window. Her aunt's car was gone. She'd probably already headed to the store for her weekly grocery trip.

She drank in the beautiful countryside just across the road. Full, lush trees blanketed the hillside and seemed to roll like waves atop the ground and along the sky. She could see Nick and Addy's house and barn just before the tree line. Endless rows of wooden fences spread out before her eyes with more cows than she could count grazing in the fields.

Running her fingers through her matted hair, an overwhelming sense of refreshment welled within her. She'd slept the whole night without a nightmare. No would-be rapist threatening her. No father walking out. For the first time in weeks, she felt rested. *I wonder if Gracie's prayer had anything to do with it.* She blinked as she pushed the thought aside.

Normally she'd head straight to the shower and get ready

for her day before heading to the kitchen for coffee and breakfast. But she loved to sit on the back deck and look out at her aunt's full vegetable and herb garden. The flower garden was equally amazing, bursting in reds, yellows, whites, and purples. She'd grown to need the time she spent basking in the early morning's slight breeze while she sipped her java. If she waited until after a shower, the sun would be too hot to enjoy the coffee on the deck. She grabbed the bright pink fuzzy robe her aunt had given her as a hand-me-down and slipped into it.

Knowing her uncle was most likely watching one of the morning news shows or playing on his Wii, Melody traipsed down the stairs then hollered down the hall, "Uncle Roy, I can't believe I slept this late."

She walked into the living room. He was sitting in his recliner watching a news show, just as she expected. But he was resting at an odd angle, slightly hunched to one side with his elbow resting on the arm of the chair and his hand cupping the side of his face.

Her heartbeat quickened, and her stomach churned at the pensive expression on his face. "Uncle Roy, are you all right?"

He tried to look up at her, but his eyes squinted, and he didn't seem to have the strength to lift his chin. "My head. . ." His words slurred, and his mouth seemed to drag on one side.

Panic welled within her, but she forced herself to remain calm. She raced into the kitchen, grabbed the phone, and dialed 911. The dispatcher answered.

"I believe my uncle is having a stroke." Melody could hear the anxiety in her voice even as she tried to remain steady. As she relayed their address to the woman, Melody grabbed a plastic bag from under the sink. The woman told her he could start vomiting at any moment. She needed to watch to be sure he didn't choke.

The thought of it spurred a sob within her chest. She sucked in her breath, willing herself to stay in control of her emotions. Racing back into the living area, her heart pounded at the sight of Uncle Roy slumped farther in the chair. She pushed back the recliner to shift him in what appeared to be a more comfortable position.

The dispatcher continued to ask her what her uncle was doing, when his eyes opened wider as if in panic. She placed the bag under his mouth just before he started to vomit. Tears pooled in her eyes, and she tried to swallow them back as she asked the dispatcher, "How much longer until they'll be here?"

"Just a few more minutes, honey," the woman tried to reassure her. She kept talking, but Melody only heard a jumbling of words from the woman.

Seconds seemed like hours. Melody felt so helpless, so out of control. There was nothing she could do to help her uncle. He kept trying to talk to her, and Melody tried to understand what he said, but his words slurred together; plus the dispatcher continued to ask questions and make comments.

Melody sat close to him, watching to be sure he didn't vomit again and choke, or fall and hurt himself worse, or stop breathing. She could tell his body continued to tighten, and she knew at any moment he could pass out or die.

The thought of him dying sent a wave of fear and nausea through her body. She loved this man. He'd been the only consistent male in her life. He'd always been good and caring and fun. She didn't want him to die.

She heard the distant sound of sirens, and relief washed over her. The piercing noise grew closer, and she looked out the front bay window. She saw the ambulance approaching and looked back at her uncle. "Help is coming, Uncle Roy. Hang on. They're coming."

The ambulance pulled into the driveway, and two men jumped out of the front. They dashed around the back of the vehicle and pulled out a gurney. Melody swung open the front door, waving them inside. The older, gray-haired one came through the door. "Where is he, ma'am?"

As he spoke, his gaze scanned the room for her uncle. She pointed to the recliner, but he was already rushing to him. The younger man pushed inside the door, and the two of them began to assess her uncle.

Her body began to shake with relief that they were there but also with fear they couldn't help him. Realizing she needed to call her aunt, she ran back to her bedroom and grabbed her cell phone off the nightstand.

She pushed her aunt's number as she made her way back to the living room. They had already loaded Uncle Roy onto the gurney and were wheeling him out the front door.

"I'm going with you," she hollered. The younger man nodded for her to come on.

"What's going on?" Her aunt's voice sounded over the phone. Melody hadn't realized the line connected. Before she could respond, her aunt continued, "Are those sirens in the background? Melody, are you there?"

"Yes, Aunt Renee." Melody tried to sound calm as she stepped up into the back of the ambulance. Just realizing she wasn't dressed but in her pajamas and pink robe, she scrunched her face. She wasn't immodest, and she hadn't had time to dress. Her uncle's health was most important.

"What's going on?"

"It's Uncle Roy." Melody sat on the benchlike seat in the back of the ambulance while the older emergency technician connected him to a machine. "I think he's having a stroke."

"What?" Aunt Renee's voice heightened, and Melody knew her aunt was going to panic.

"We're on our way to the hospital. Meet us there."

"I'm coming," her aunt said. Crackles and rustling sounded over the line, as Aunt Renee must have forgotten to push the END button on the phone. Melody could hear the beeping of the car when she opened the door. Her aunt's audible prayer sounded over the line. "Oh dear Jesus, please heavenly Lord, don't take Roy. Not yet. . ."

Melody pushed the END button on her phone and shoved it deep into the robe's pocket. She looked down at her uncle. In the midst of all that was happening in his body, his face still glowed of a peace she didn't understand. But his body seemed to still be tightening. He looked to be completely paralyzed on one side.

And there was nothing she could do to help him.

She'd tried to make him comfortable. She'd kept him from vomiting all over himself. She'd called the ambulance. But she couldn't heal him. She couldn't make him better. She had absolutely no control, and she hated it.

❧

"Come on, son. We've got to go!"

Noting the urgency in his dad's voice, Drew tossed the shovel against the barn wall and jogged to his dad. He pulled off his gloves and hopped into the cab of the truck as his dad started the engine. "What's going on?"

"Gotta get to the hospital."

A myriad of reasons to rush to the hospital whizzed through his mind. His mother was most likely at the grocery store with Renee. Could they have had a wreck? Did something happen on the farm to one of his friends? Did Melody get hurt trying to fix a vehicle? "What happened?"

"Roy's had a stroke."

"How? When?"

"Apparently Melody woke up and found him hunched over in his recliner. She called the ambulance and got them there in a hurry." The truck bounced through a large pothole in the road, but his dad didn't slow down. "But your mom doesn't know if he's all right yet or not. They're at the hospital. Half the church is already there praying."

Drew stared out the windshield. Within moments, trees and fields gave way to buildings and streetlights. They passed a subdivision, then a gas station, a couple of fast-food restaurants, and then a grocery store. Finally, they made it to the hospital. Drew recognized several of the cars and trucks in the emergency parking lot. He saw Doris shuffling to the door after having just had hip replacement surgery only two months before. Her sisters, Joanne, Maggie, and Betty hustled behind her, fussing that she needed to slow down.

He was thankful for the outpouring of love his church family was sure to drape over Renee and the family. Many prayers would storm heaven's gates for Roy's recovery. But Drew still worried about what was happening at that moment.

Without a word, he and his dad rushed into the emergency

room. His mom saw them, ran to them, and grabbed her father in a hug. She released him then gripped Drew's hand. "He's going to be okay."

Tears streamed down her face, and a smile brightened her lips. She squeezed Drew's hand then grabbed his father's hand with her other one. "He had what's called an ischemic stroke, and they were able to give him some medicine." His mother released their hands and called over to one of their church friends, "Anita, what did the doctor say that medicine was called?"

"Tissue plasminogen activator."

His mom turned back toward Drew and his dad. She laughed and patted his dad's chest. "What she said. But the important thing is he's going to be okay. They have to watch him for bleeding, but his prognosis is good."

"God is so good." His dad's praise was barely above a whisper as he swiped his hand down the entirety of his face.

"Your buddy's going to be okay." His mom nudged his dad's shoulder. "Come sit down."

Not ready to have a seat, Drew watched as his parents sat beside their pastor and his wife, Joan. They'd spent far too much time in a hospital with Joan having battled cancer in two separate parts of her body over the last few years. God had mercifully healed her both times.

Drew scanned the room. He felt humbled by the care and concern his church displayed. Behind him he could hear some of the ladies making a calendar of who would prepare which meals for the family and on what days. He knew his dad and several of the other men would probably argue over who would have the privilege of mowing Roy's one-acre yard.

On the far side of the room, Drew spotted Melody

wearing a bright pink robe. Her hair stuck out at odd angles all over her head. She had her elbows propped against her knees, and her face was buried in her hands. Sweet, quiet Wanda sat beside her with one hand on Melody's back.

Feeling prodded by the Holy Spirit, he made his way to them. Wanda stood up slowly. "Here, honey. I'll let you sit here. I've missed my morning medicine, and I need to go take it."

Hesitantly, Drew sat beside Melody. She didn't move, aside from the rising and falling of her back. He clasped his hands in front of him. Should he touch her back as Wanda had? Would she be offended? She most definitely didn't seem to be the kind of girl who would appreciate an uninvited touch of reassurance.

His mind kept imagining what she must have felt walking into the living room to Roy having a stroke. She must have been so afraid, and it must have seemed like forever until the ambulance arrived. He didn't even want to think about how it would feel to fear someone he loved might die before help could arrive.

If it were him, he would be on his knees in prayer, clinging to God for help, wisdom, and comfort. But Melody didn't have that.

He looked at her robe and hair again. It was obvious she had just awakened when it happened. She probably hadn't eaten or brushed her teeth. He knew she must feel every bit as uncomfortable as she was afraid.

No matter what she thought of him, he had to show her that he cared. He had to at least try to comfort her. Slowly, he wrapped his arm around her and squeezed her shoulder. "I'm sorry, Melody."

She turned toward him, buried her face in his chest, and wrapped both arms around him. Her back heaved with the sobs she seemed no longer able to hold back. He pulled her closer and patted her back. Every protective urge he'd ever felt prickled his skin. He'd do anything to make her feel better, to assure her he'd do everything in his power to keep her from pain.

Without thinking, he lowered his lips to the top of her head. Though tangled, her hair was still soft and smelled of shampoo. He raked his fingers through a portion of the long hair against her back. "It's okay, Melody."

She continued to cry, and he didn't let her go. He'd hold her for the rest of his life if she'd let him. Anything to take the tears away from this beautiful, strong, competitive, almost always difficult creature.

A shadow fell over him, and he looked up and saw Renee. She bent over and rubbed the back of Melody's head. "You did good, honey. Why don't you let Drew take you home to change?"

To his surprise, Melody lifted her head and nodded. She stood, and Drew got up and placed his hand in the small of her back. He still felt the need to protect her.

Renee's eyes were red rimmed and her nose was puffy from tears that had shifted from fear to rejoicing. She touched Drew's shoulder. "Please stay with her a little while."

Drew nodded. He wouldn't have a problem with that. He had no intention of leaving Melody alone. After getting the keys from his dad, he guided her to the truck, opened the door for her, then raced around to the driver's side and got in. They didn't speak as he drove to Roy and Renee's house. He pulled into the driveway and parked. Looking over at her, he noted her furrowed brows as she bit her bottom lip. He knew she was remembering having left there only a few hours before in an ambulance.

Once he got her out of the truck and into the house, he tried to lighten the tension she felt. "You go get cleaned up, and I'll find something for us to eat." He looked at the clock. "It's almost one o'clock. I bet you're starving. I know I am."

She didn't say anything as she puttered down the hall and up the stairs. A few moments later, he heard water running in the shower. He rummaged through the refrigerator to see what Renee had that he could fix for lunch. The pickings were slim, as she had been going to the grocery store when Roy had the stroke.

He found a little bit of sliced turkey and bread. He made a couple of sandwiches then cut apple slices and put them on two plates. Spying some packaged chocolate chip cookies, he put a few on each plate as well. Not sure what she'd drink, he decided he'd let her get that herself when she was ready.

She finally made it to the kitchen wearing cutoff sweatpants and a T-shirt. Her hair was tied in a knot at the back of her head, and her face was scrubbed clean. To his surprise, her bare feet exposed toenails painted a bright pinkish orange color with a small white flower on her big toenails. He wondered if his sister had something to do with that.

He smiled when she looked up at him. "Hey. I made us some lunch. I wasn't sure what you'd want to drink."

She opened the refrigerator and grabbed a soft drink. Popping the top, she nodded as she sat down in the chair across from his. "Thanks, Drew."

They didn't talk as they ate their sandwiches, apples, and cookies, but Drew noted that she did eat. In fact, she ate everything on her plate. She must have been starving. She stared off into space, and Drew prayed for the right words to say to her.

"It was good you got Roy to the hospital so quickly."

She nodded.

"They believe he's going to make a full recovery."

She gazed at Drew. Her eyes pooled with tears. "I was so scared. I thought he was going to die right there in the living room. I didn't know what to do."

"You did exactly what you were supposed to do."

She shook her head. "But I couldn't help him. Not really. I could make him comfortable and keep him from vomiting all over himself, but I couldn't fix him. I couldn't make him better. I couldn't control—" Her voice broke, and she sucked in a deep breath. She picked up a paper towel and patted her eyes.

Drew reached across the table and patted her hand. "Melody, you did everything right. Just like Renee said, you did good."

Melody shook her head. "I had no control."

Drew furrowed his eyebrows, beginning to see the basis of Melody's need to be the best for the first time. "None of us do. Not really."

eight

The next morning Drew woke up long before the sun. Several of his friends were supposed to come over to start framing his house. With spending the afternoon with Melody and most of the evening at the hospital, he'd forgotten to tell them they'd wait until next week.

He started down the stairs to get the coffee brewing before his dad woke up. The strong aroma filled his nostrils before he made it into the kitchen. He saw his dad already dressed in work clothes and boots, sitting at the table with a steaming mug pressed against his lips. He set the mug down and looked at Drew. "'Bout time you got up, son. I thought we had a house to frame today."

Drew furrowed his eyebrows. "Dad, I just assumed we'd wait. What with Roy's stroke yesterday, and—I'm sure no one is going to show up."

"I guess I'm no one," Nick's deep voice sounded from inside the pantry. He held a dainty, rose-framed container of sugar in his left hand and his fish-decorated coffee cup in his right.

Drew grinned at how ridiculous his oversized friend looked pouring sugar from that container into the oversized mug. "Nick, what are you doing here? You should be with your dad."

Nick guffawed. "Are you kidding? Dad's mad as a hornet that he couldn't be here. You know how the man is. He was carrying on, even while slurring his words, that he was slacking on his part."

Drew pursed his lips. He knew Nick was probably telling the truth about that. Roy never shirked on a task he'd told someone he'd do. Nick's and Drew's dads had raised both of them to be that way. If a person told someone they were going to do something they had better do it. *A man's only as good as his word.* He'd heard Roy and his dad say those words so many times they used to make him sick.

Drew scratched at the stubble on his jaw. "Well, I think the three of us will have our work cut out for us. Won't be easy framing the house with just us."

"Now why would you think that?" His dad scooted his chair back and leaned his arm against the table. "Mike and his dad and brother, as well as about five guys from church, are all coming to help get that house framed. It's just a little ranch house. We'll have it done by the end of the day."

Drew's jaw dropped. "They're all coming?" He scratched his head. "I just assumed—I mean, Roy had a stroke, and we all lost a good part of a day's work on the farm." He nodded toward Nick. "Not that we minded. You know Roy's health comes first."

Nick lifted his hand to stop Drew's words. "Enough of that, sleeping beauty."

Drew looked down, noting that he still wore the basketball shorts and white T-shirt he'd worn to bed.

Nick shooed him with his hand. "Just get your tail on up those steps and get ready. We've got a house to frame."

Drew turned and climbed the first two steps. He looked back at Nick. "Roy's really doing good?"

Nick swallowed hard, and Drew knew yesterday had

nearly scared the life out of him. Drew couldn't imagine how he'd feel if it had been his dad lying in that hospital bed. It was bad enough that it was Roy. He was like an uncle to Drew.

Nick nodded. "He really is. I've already talked to Mom this morning." He cleared his throat, probably warding off a show of emotion. "We're very thankful."

"How 'bout Melody? She was still pretty shook up when I left yesterday."

"Melody is so hard to figure out." Nick leaned against the pantry door. "Usually she has something to say or argues about everything. But she was real quiet yesterday. I can't tell what's going on in her head."

Drew nodded then headed back up the steps. Melody was a hard one to read. No doubt about that. But yesterday he felt he'd seen a little insight into her "problem."

The woman needed to be in control. It was no wonder she hadn't accepted God as her Savior. Becoming a Christian was all about faith and being willing to give up control of her life to follow Jesus. As long as Melody clung to being in control of her life, she could never accept Christ.

Drew's heart felt heavy. She had to know she didn't really have control of anything. She had to see it in her life and in nature. There was no controlling a tornado or a flash flood. She couldn't decide who was willing to seek her mechanical abilities or even how other people drove their cars. Yesterday, she momentarily lost control at the hospital and allowed him to comfort her with a hug and kind words—something he knew she would normally never do.

God, help her to see that the most control she will ever have over her life or circumstances is when she gives it up to You. . .when she has faith that You will give her peace and hope in whatever life brings her.

Drew sighed as he realized anew what a terrible witness he had been. His competitive spirit was really just that—a competitive spirit. He loved to battle and win. And he had to admit he was really not very good at losing at all. It was actually something he really needed to work on—losing gracefully.

But his competitive nature wasn't about him controlling the world around him. He *wanted* to win, but Melody *needed* to. Realizing the difference between them weighed his heart with conviction about the way he'd allowed his pride to get wrapped up in their ridiculous battles.

God, forgive me. Draw Melody to You. Whatever it takes, may she give her life to You.

꙳

The doorbell rang, and Melody hopped off the couch and opened the front door. A woman from the church stood on the porch with several deli sandwiches in her hands. "Hi. I brought some lunch."

Melody forced herself to smile to be polite. They'd already had so many visitors, and they had more food than they'd be able to eat in a week. More than anything, Melody just wanted to have a little time alone. She waved to the woman. "Come on in."

"Thanks, Melody." The woman walked through the living room and into the kitchen and placed the sandwiches on the table. She extended her hand. "I'm Sheila. Can't remember if we formally met."

"And I guess you already know I'm Melody."

"Is that Sheila?" Aunt Renee called from the back of the

house. She walked into the kitchen and gave Sheila a quick hug. "Roy's resting. Thanks so much for bringing us lunch."

"I didn't have time to cook, as I have to be at work in thirty minutes, but I was sure to pick up food I know Roy can eat."

Aunt Renee turned toward Melody. "Sheila's a nurse."

Melody took in the pastel-flowered nurse uniform top and blue pants. "I can tell."

Sheila looked at her watch. "I better be going. Tell Roy we're praying for him." Sheila walked back to the front door. "Oh. . .I almost forgot. Sarah gave this to me at youth last night and asked me to give it to you." She pulled a homemade card out of her purse.

Aunt Renee chuckled. "The girl got her nose out of a book long enough to make him a card?"

"Yep."

"That was so sweet of her."

"She's a good kid." Sheila raised her hand. "I gotta go. I'll see you later."

Aunt Renee shut the door behind her. She opened the card and read the contents to Melody. The teenager's sentiments were kind and heartfelt, and her aunt had to brush a tear out of her eye. "Will you put this on the table with the others? It will make Roy's day to see all these things once he wakes up."

Aunt Renee gave the card to Melody then gripped her free hand. "I'm so thankful our Roy is going to be okay."

Afraid her emotions would get the best of her again, she looked away and mumbled, "Me, too."

Melody walked into the dining room, taking in the magnitude of cards her aunt had stood up on the table.

Several flowers sat around the room, most of them either various shades of blue or adorned with blue ribbon. It was obvious his church family understood Uncle Roy's fanatical feelings about the University of Kentucky Wildcat basketball team. The kindness shown by his church family would overwhelm him once he was able to see all they'd done.

And the food! In addition to the cold cuts and baked dishes, fresh vegetables and fruits, several people had also brought over dishes just for her and Aunt Renee: desserts rich in chocolate that they were supposed to indulge in whenever Uncle Roy took a nap.

Her cell phone buzzed in her front pocket. She pulled it out and looked at the number on the screen. It was her mom. Melody had called her the night before to tell her about Uncle Roy, but she'd gotten the voice mail and had only been able to leave a message. It had been so long since Melody talked to her. Her heart raced with a need to hear her mom's live voice, to know she was all right. She pushed the TALK button. "Hello, Mom."

"Hi, Melody. I got your message. How is Roy?"

"He's doing good. They were able to get him medicine at the right time. He should make a full recovery."

"That's great."

Melody could hear her mother's husband talking in the background. She couldn't make out what he was saying, but he sounded frustrated. Melody sucked in her breath. She really didn't like that man. "How have you been, Mom?"

Her voice sounded muffled, and Melody assumed her mother had put her hand over the phone so Melody couldn't hear her talking to her husband. It was apparent she was more concerned with getting back to her new husband than she was about her brother-in-law's health. Or talking with her only daughter. Their relationship, as strained as it had been all the years after her dad walked out, seemed to get worse instead of better. Melody wondered if it was easier for her mother to simply put all of the painful past behind her and start anew with the new guy.

Her mother's voice sounded again. "I'm sorry, Melody. Frank and I were just getting ready to head to town. I'll talk to you later."

Before Melody could respond, her mother hung up. She sucked in a deep breath and bit her bottom lip as she pulled the phone away from her ear and clicked it off. She would not focus on her lack of a relationship with her mother. She bit her lip harder. She refused to feel sorry for herself.

Aunt Renee walked into the dining room. She held a piece of paper in her hand. "Melody, could you do me a big favor?"

Grateful for the opportunity to think of something else, she turned toward her aunt. "Absolutely. Anything."

"You know I didn't get to finish my grocery trip, and even though I don't think we'll need much food for a while. . ."

Melody chuckled. "I think you're right about that."

"We still need toilet paper and toothpaste and several other things. Would you be willing to go for me?" She held out the paper. "Addy offered to go, but I thought you might like to get out of the house for a while."

Melody nodded. "Of course I'll go." She was glad for the excuse to go somewhere. When AJ insisted she not come in to work today, she'd been grateful for his kindness, but she also knew that sitting around the house would make her feel antsy. She'd want to be working on something, but her tractor was ready for the tractor pull on Friday, and they'd weeded the garden two days ago. Aside from cleaning the house, which she did not like the idea of doing, and it didn't need it anyway, she really had too much time on her hands today. She added, "I may stop by Gracie's on the way home."

"Yes, you do that. It will do you good to get your hands on that sweet little guy."

Melody chewed the inside of her lip. Her love for Wyatt Jr. was apparent to everyone. The little guy had her wrapped around his chubby finger.

She took the list, grabbed the keys off the counter, and headed out the door. It didn't take long to get everything on her aunt's list, especially since most of it had been marked through because of all the food they'd been given.

She pulled into Gracie's driveway and saw Gracie pushing Wyatt in the swing in the backyard. Melody honked, and Gracie scooped Wyatt into her arms, making him wave his chubby hand at her. Melody got out and made her way through the gate and into the backyard. "Hey. Thought I'd stop by for a minute."

"I'm so glad you did."

Wyatt leaned over, reaching his arms out to Melody. She cooed at the baby and took him from his mom. "Come here, you rotten stink."

Wyatt cackled and grabbed for the strands of her hair that had fallen out of her ponytail. Pushing them behind her ear, she Eskimo kissed him. "This boy only loves me for my hair."

"I don't know about that." Gracie patted his diaper-padded bottom. "The boy knows when he's got someone hooked."

Melody tickled his neck. "That's because you're a smart boy, aren't you?"

Gracie motioned toward the back door. "Come inside. Let's get a glass of sweet tea."

Melody followed her then sat on the couch in the great room. She plopped Wyatt on her lap so that he was facing her. He reached for the buttons on her shirt, and Melody picked up his oversized key ring off the end table and handed it to him.

"How's Roy doing?" Gracie walked into the room, handed her a glass, then sat on the love seat.

"He's doing remarkably well. He should make a full recovery." She grinned. "He's even planning to go to the tractor pull."

"Praise God!" Gracie practically shouted through the room. Little Wyatt looked at his mother as if she'd lost her mind. She grabbed his arm and lifted it in the air. "Say 'Praise God,' my little man."

Today, Gracie's outburst didn't upset Melody. She was too overwhelmed to be aggravated. Wyatt cackled, and Melody spied something in his mouth. "Uh-oh, buddy, what's in your mouth?"

Gracie squealed. "Did you see it?" She pulled down on Wyatt's lower lip. "A tooth!"

"What!" Wyatt shook his head to get his mother's finger away from his lip. Melody put her finger on his mouth to try to get another look. He bit down, and she felt the small, hard tooth. "Wyatt Jr." She lifted the baby in the air. "You're not allowed to get teeth." She gently twisted him back and forth. "You're supposed to stay a baby." He cooed, and slobber oozed out of his mouth and hit Melody on the forehead.

She brought him down back to her lap, and Gracie howled. She handed Melody a cloth diaper. "Well, that's what he thinks about that."

Melody wiped her forehead. "I guess so." She handed the toy keys back to Wyatt, and he shoved them into his mouth. Melody frowned. "Seriously though, he's growing up so fast."

Gracie sighed. "Believe me, I know it." She swatted Melody's arm. "Don't worry. I'm sure you'll have plenty of babies of your own."

Melody snorted. "I doubt that."

"Why? Don't you think you'll get married?"

Melody scrunched her nose. She'd always thought she'd never in a million years want to get married, but having watched her aunt take care of her uncle since his stroke and watching him respond to her—something had changed inside her. Uncle Roy and Aunt Renee, Drew's parents, Wyatt and Gracie—since moving to River Run, Melody had witnessed some good marriages. From everything she'd seen between Addy and Nick, they would be very happy as well. If she could have a marriage like that, then maybe she wouldn't mind so much.

The feel of Drew's strong arms around her flooded her mind and rushed through her. She'd felt protected and cared for. When he'd kissed her head, though she knew it was in innocence, for a moment, she'd wondered what it would be like to feel his lips against hers. The idea of it scared her, and she pushed the thought away.

She looked at her friend, who still waited for her to answer. She shook her head. "No. I've never thought I would get married."

nine

Drew inhaled the sweet aroma of diesel engine smoke and grease and even a dabbling of sweat. Nearly the whole town had come out for the tractor pull and fireworks. In addition to the vending machines, the women's auxiliary had set up several portable, inflatable games. There were two with slides, one made like a cage for the kids to jump in, and another that was an obstacle course. The high school cheerleaders had set up a face-painting tent. They even had several people who'd set up tents to sell all kinds of crafts—fancy pillows and quilts, knickknacks, and belt buckles. There was even a Christmas decorations tent—on the Fourth of July! The tractor pull was becoming a town festival of its own.

With his tractor already pulled up to the starting line, he looked around for Melody and her tractor. As luck would have it, she was one of the final two tractors, and he'd have to race her.

Different places raced different ways. Mostly people simply timed each tractor, and the winner took all, but Drew liked the way River Run did it.

Tractors raced against time the first round. They'd take turns driving the one hundred meters to see which two tractors could pull their sled the fastest. At the end, the top two tractors would race each other for the ultimate prize: a big ol' trophy, a $250 gift certificate to Wyatt's Hardware Store, and bragging rights for a year.

Granted, he'd seen many a fellow make it to the finals with a good time in the first round but then have to drop out because their engine blew or something else broke on his tractor. But if a guy built his tractor tough enough, as Drew always did, it would be able to withstand the challenge. Melody's had come through looking pretty good as well.

And tonight, she would come out the overall victor.

It was still hard on his pride to think about it, and in his mind, he knew that his losing wasn't going to make Melody see the need to give her feigned control of her life over to God. But maybe if she saw him lose and handle it the way he should, the way Mike always handled loss, then maybe she'd see that Drew didn't have to win at everything. She needed to see there were more important things in his life than taking home the prize.

Mike walked up to him and grabbed his hand in a firm handshake. "I still can't believe it's going to be you against Melody for the championship."

"I know. It's crazy, isn't it?"

Mike raised his eyebrows. "I'll tell you what it is. That woman's your match." He extended his arms. "Never in my wildest dreams would I have ever imagined a person, let alone a girl, would be able to get the best of Drew Wilson." He pointed to a stream of smoke. "And yet, here she comes."

Drew saw Melody driving around the tractor of a guy from another county. She'd fixed up Roy's old John Deere just as Drew expected. Even from a distance he could tell she'd done a lot of work to the old girl.

A slow smile bowed his lips. Melody had done a good job. She truly was quite the mechanic. In a way he couldn't quite explain, Drew was kind of proud of her.

"Just so you know, and it's no offense"—Mike patted Drew's shoulder—"but I'm betting on Melody."

Drew noted the gleam in Mike's eye, and he knew his friend was only trying to mess around with him. But for the slightest moment, Drew's competitive pride reared up within him, and he felt the urge to jump on his tractor seat and blow Roy's old tractor out of the fairgrounds. Shaking off the feeling, he returned the pat on Mike's shoulder, only a little firmer than Mike must have expected, because he flinched under the pat. "She's exactly who'd I'd put my money on."

Mike frowned, but Drew nodded to his friend then turned his attention to Melody. She pulled up to the starting line and stepped down from the seat. He nodded to his friend. "Excuse me, Mike. I'm going to go wish my rival good luck. In a matter of speaking, anyway."

Drew walked toward Melody. He didn't believe in luck, and he never uttered the words to his opponents, but he wanted to be able to say something to Melody before their race.

She had the helmet stuck under her arm as she looked over the outside of her tractor. He grinned as he couldn't help but admit she looked kind of cute in Nick's much-too-big-for-her racing garb. He extended his hand to her. "Hey. I just wanted to wish you luck."

She pursed her lips and glared up at him. "I didn't think you'd believe in luck."

Caught off guard, he stepped back and dropped his hand. "You're right. I don't. But I wanted to—"

Fire lit her eyes, and she moved toward him like a rabid dog about to attack. "Look, Drew. Don't try to be nice to me so you can knock me off my game and win this championship." She poked him in the chest with her finger. "You're just going to have to take being beaten by a girl."

With a huff, she walked away from him and stuck her helmet on her head.

Aggravation streamed through him. The woman never gave him a break. Never. She always thought the worst of him. No matter what he did. He'd tried over and over to be kind to that headstrong, two-bit polecat, but she simply would not have it.

He strode toward his own tractor. Grabbing his helmet, he stared at his nemesis. He shoved it on his head and tapped the top to be sure it was in place. *Little lady, you're going to eat my dust.*

❧

Melody stepped up and into the seat of the John Deere. She had no idea why she had been mean to Drew. Just edgy. The last few days had her in a whirlwind of frustration. She was confused about everything in life. But she shouldn't have snapped at him like that.

He had been so kind to her the day he brought her home from the hospital. She knew then that he had a good heart. Truthfully, deep in her gut, she'd known it long before then. His need to always come out on top had just struck a chord somewhere down deep inside, and she'd done everything she could to show him up.

She looked toward the bleachers. Uncle Roy had insisted on coming to the tractor pull. He still didn't have all his strength in his hand, and his face still fell ever so slightly on the left side. His speech slurred, but she could understand everything he said. Since his right hand hadn't been affected, he still played his Wii, which made Melody chuckle. He didn't play it quite as much, as he needed rest, and Aunt Renee made him rest. But Melody knew as soon as he could he'd drive them crazy with the video game once again.

Fearing he'd not be able to sit without back support the whole time, Aunt Renee brought two folding chairs for them to sit in. She'd set them up close to the bleachers, as Uncle Roy loved to chat with everyone who passed his way.

Tonight he didn't have any trouble finding people to talk to him. Melody watched as one person after another stopped to shake his hand or give him a hug. First, it was Cindy and Tricia. Melody thought of them as the Bobbsey twins. Everywhere they went, they went together.

Then it was Lana. Then another lady. Melody tried to remember her name. The woman's husband wore a long beard, white as snow, and he drove an old historical train for tourists. He was the most welcoming man she'd ever met in her life, practically squealing, "Well hello, Melody!" each time he saw her. She snapped her fingers. *Sue.* That was the woman's name.

Melody's attention was diverted as Drew hopped onto his tractor seat. She wanted him to look over at her. She needed to apologize, but he kept his gaze straight ahead. He looked tense and furious. She couldn't be sure, but she imagined that if he took off that helmet the veins in his neck and forehead would be bulging with fury.

The track was ready. She knew they were about to start, and she needed to get her mind off Uncle Roy and off Drew Wilson and onto the race. She looked at the finish line. Surprisingly, she didn't care much about this race. She just wanted to be done with it.

AJ signaled for her to let him know if she was ready.

After giving a thumbs-up, she glanced once more back at Uncle Roy. Another woman from the church, Rhonda, was bent over, giving him a hug.

Rhonda had confused Melody since the first time she met her. Ten years before, Rhonda lost her sixteen-year-old daughter to a heart defect. It was sudden and unexpected, and when Rhonda talked of the girl it was obvious she had been a pride and joy to her and her husband.

What Melody didn't understand was that despite the loss, Rhonda was filled with joy. She headed up the kitchen ministry at Uncle Roy and Aunt Renee's church, organizing the meals that were taken to families in the church who were in crisis, organizing Thanksgiving and Christmas dinners for families in the community in need, even cooking dinner every Wednesday evening before church services.

Melody simply didn't understand the woman. Gracie's little boy, Wyatt, wasn't even Melody's son, but if God took him, she would be devastated. Rhonda had the right to be devastated.

"I have told you these things, so that in me you may have peace. In this world you will have trouble. But take heart! I have overcome the world."

The scripture the preacher had spoken about filtered through her mind. She'd gone home and searched in her aunt's Bible for that scripture, memorizing it because it bothered her so much.

Old English lessons washed through her thoughts. She'd taken many an extra lesson as she'd struggled so badly with reading in school. Sentences ending in a period were a statement or a declaration. *"In this world you will have trouble,"* and *"I have overcome the world."* They were declarations made by Jesus. *"But take heart!"* It was written with an exclamation point. Jesus was exclaiming or shouting to the people, *"Take heart!" Don't give up. Don't give in.*

I'm not supposed to give up. Not supposed to give in.

But why do so many bad things happen? Horrible things? Why doesn't God stop them? Why don't You stop them, God?

She peered at Rhonda. Tears welled in her eyes as the woman reached down to hug her aunt. Rhonda had lost her daughter. Her child. It didn't seem fair. Didn't seem right. Why? Because bad things happen. But Rhonda didn't give up. She didn't give in.

Humbled to her core, Melody's view of God began to shift. Bonnie wasn't being punished with gnarled hands. She was able to show love and kindness despite continuous pain. Gracie wasn't being ridiculous with her constant conversations with and about God. She trusted Him with every aspect of her life.

The gunshot sounded, signaling the start of the race. Drew's tractor shot forward, but Melody didn't care. She closed her eyes and allowed the tears to stream down her cheeks. *Forgive me, God. I am a sinner. Please accept me anyway. I long for what Gracie and Uncle Roy and Aunt Renee and Bonnie and Rhonda have—for what they have with You.*

She opened her eyes. The heavens didn't part, and she didn't see Jesus in the sky, but she knew she was different. Something inside her had changed.

Looking ahead, she saw that Drew had already reached the finish line. He jumped off the tractor, threw off his helmet, and let the loudest whoop she'd ever heard peal through the air.

He raced the full one hundred meters back, pointing

both index fingers at her. "Take that, little lady. Now, get off your pedestal, and—"

"Drew, I don't even care about the race." She jumped down from the tractor, stood on tiptoes, and wrapped her arms around him in a quick hug. "I've accepted Jesus into my heart."

Drew's eyes seemed to bulge out of their sockets as he took a step back. "What?"

"I'm a Christian." She clapped her hands. For the first time in her life, all dressed in protective gear with grease smearing her face and her hair knotted up to fit a helmet, she felt like a giddy schoolgirl. "Aren't you excited?"

Before Drew could respond, AJ walked toward them holding a microphone in one hand and the trophy in the other. "Same ending as last year, folks. This year's tractor pull winner is—"

Melody pushed Drew toward AJ. "Run over there and get your trophy." She waved toward her aunt and uncle. Confused expressions marked their faces and she could hardly wait to tell them what had happened.

"Melody." Drew tried to step toward her. Sadness wrapped his face for no reason she could understand. This was the happiest day of her life.

She shooed him away. "Go on. Get your trophy. I've got to talk to Uncle Roy and Aunt Renee."

Throwing her helmet on the ground, she rushed to her aunt and uncle.

"Melody, what happened?" Uncle Roy asked as she wrapped her arms around his neck.

"Is the tractor not working right?" asked Aunt Renee.

New tears swept down her cheeks as she shook her

head. "No. Everything is fine. Everything is wonderful. I've accepted Jesus."

"You what?" Aunt Renee's eyebrows lifted.

"You did?" Uncle Roy smiled.

"Did I just hear correctly?" Gracie hollered as she stepped toward Melody. "You accepted Jesus?"

Melody nodded, and Gracie smashed her with the tightest hug she'd ever experienced.

"Melody's a Christian!" Addy's voice sounded from the bleachers three seats behind them.

"I heard," Nick said. Melody giggled as he tried to make his way down the bleachers to her.

"Praise the Lord," said someone.

"God is so good," said another.

"He doesn't want any to perish," responded yet another.

"I knew you were going to come over to the light side," Nick said as he towered over her. "Now come give Cousin Nick a proper hug."

Before Melody could protest, Nick threw her over his shoulder as he had done when he was a teen and she was a girl. He twirled around several times then plopped her back on her feet. When she was little, he'd let her go just to see her wobble around then fall to the ground. This time he held her in a bear hug. "I'm so happy for you."

Allowing a peace that goes beyond understanding to envelop her whole being, she sucked in a long breath. "Me, too."

ten

Drew was a dog. He was lower than a dog. He was the scum on the bottom of the dog's paw. He wasn't even worthy to be on the bottom of the dog's paw. He covered his face with his hands. He couldn't believe he had acted that way.

Standing on his own farm, mending his own fence several days after the tractor pull, and his face still warmed with embarrassment at the memory of it. *God, You even told me to let it go, to show her care and encouragement, to not be so consumed with winning, but like always, my pride got the best of me.*

He'd wanted to dig a hole and hide inside it when AJ announced Drew the ultimate winner of the tractor pull and handed him the trophy. Almost no one in the stands seemed to give a care about his win. Everyone he knew surrounded Melody, congratulating her, while everyone else looked down at her, confused by what had happened.

I should have just thrown that trophy on the ground and rushed over to give her a hug like the others. But he hadn't. Shame had wrapped itself around him, and Drew grabbed the trophy, loaded up his tractor, and headed straight home. Conviction at his behavior had eaten him alive ever since.

He finished hammering the broken fence post back in place then looked at the cows that grazed beside him. Thinking he'd brought a treat, several made their way toward him when he jumped inside the fence. He watched as one of them lifted her head. Her mouth was full of grass, and she chomped at it with no apparent concern in the world.

"Life's pretty easy for a cow." He reached out and petted her nose. Her calf moved close to her and grabbed hold of one of her teats. The cow didn't so much as take an extra blink. She didn't have to worry about pride or embarrassment or admitting she was wrong. She just had to eat and feed her calf.

"You need to talk to her."

Drew didn't move at the sound of his dad's voice behind him. He'd heard someone walking up. He figured it was either his mom or dad coming to give him a bit of advice. He continued to stare at the cow and her calf. "I know."

"Waiting around isn't going to make it any easier."

He twisted around and looked at his dad. "Boy, don't I know it. I haven't slept in three days. I'm humiliated even out here all by myself, just me and my cows." He gripped the fence post. "Her salvation is the best thing in the world. I'm happy for her and thankful to God, and I can't even tell her."

"Sure you can. You've had to eat dirt before."

Drew laughed at the grin that spread across his dad's face. He was definitely right about that. On more than one occasion in his life Drew had been overzealous about a competition and ended up landing face-first on the losing side of embarrassment. But it had been awhile since he'd drunk from that bitter cup, and it didn't taste so great going down. "I know. I'm just not sure how to do it."

"Give her a call. It's as simple as that."

Drew let out a long breath. His dad was right. She

deserved an apology and his congratulations. And God simply wouldn't let him rest until he'd made things right. "You're right."

His dad patted his back. "I gotta get to work. See you later, son."

Drew put the hammer and extra nails in his toolbox and loaded it onto the truck. He didn't have service on his cell phone on this part of the farm. Driving closer to the house, he prayed God would give him the right words to say to Melody.

He looked down at his phone again. He had service. She'd be at work, and he probably should wait until she got home to call her, but if he didn't do it now he was afraid he'd lose his nerve.

Exhaling a long breath, he dialed AJ's number and asked to speak to Melody. She sounded confused when she answered the phone, and he assumed she probably didn't have too many people calling the shop asking to speak specifically to her.

He cleared his throat. "Hi, Melody. It's Drew."

"Hey." She sounded happy to hear from him. Something he would have never expected.

His hands started to shake, and Drew cocked his head to hold the phone against his shoulder. He stretched his arms out in front of him then wiped them against his jeans. "I need to talk to you."

His voice sounded too high, too anxious, even to his own ears. He cleared his throat again.

"Sure. Can it wait until after work?" Melody sounded chipper but anxious to get off the phone.

Drew closed his eyes. He shouldn't have called her right

now. What was he thinking? Of course he could talk to her when she got off, but where? Should he just call her again? Now that he was talking to her it just seemed wrong to say all he had to say over the phone.

An idea popped into his mind, but he wasn't sure she'd be willing to spend time alone with him at his place. He shrugged. It wouldn't hurt to ask. "Would you be willing to do a little nighttime fishing with me?"

"Absolutely. I love to fish. Where should I meet you?"

Her quick response encouraged him that she would accept his apology. At least she wasn't afraid to be alone with him. "Do you remember where my homesite is?"

"Yep. I'll meet you out there after dinner."

"Okay." He pushed the END button on his phone and stared at it. Melody probably knew as well as he did that they wouldn't catch many fish in his pond after dinnertime. They'd have to wait until closer to dark or until the early morning. But she knew they needed to talk. *I just hope she's willing to forgive me.*

略

Nearing seven o'clock in the evening, the weather was still hot and humid. Melody knew she and Drew wouldn't be catching any fish for at least another hour or two. But she and Drew had some reconciling to do, and she'd been anxious to share with him all God had shown her just in the last few days.

As they sat on the bank of his pond, she could feel in her spirit she needed to wait for Drew to do the serious talking first. She baited her hook and cast it out into the water. "So, what kind of fish you got in here?"

"Bluegill and some bass."

Melody nodded. She thought Drew might say a little more than that, but he'd been visibly nervous since she pulled up. His hand actually shook a bit when he cast his line, and the breaths he took were so big and deep, she could see his chest moving up and down as if he'd been running a race.

Trying not to make him feel any more anxious, she focused on the land before her. The pond was beautiful. Several trees towered over it on the left side of the water. But on the right bank a single strong old tree stood. It had the most enormous branch, probably twelve feet high, that was perfect for a swing. Drew had already done a lot of work to the bank just behind the house. He even had a small dock of sorts with a paddleboat tied to it.

She looked back at his house. He had the bones all up. Foundation laid. Frame in place. Outside walls up, even if they were still rough. She knew he still had to do the drywall and electric, some plumbing and other stuff, but he'd gotten a lot accomplished in the last several weeks. "The house is really coming along, Drew."

"Yep."

She blew out her breath and stared at the pond. Maybe she should be the one to start the serious talking, but her spirit still seemed to nudge her to wait. She thought about the call she'd made to her mom to tell her the good news about becoming a Christian. Her answering machine picked up. Melody left a message, but that had been two days ago, and her mom still hadn't called back. *God, I will just pray every day that she accepts You, just as Uncle Roy and Aunt Renee and everyone here prayed for me.*

"Melody, I need to talk to you." Interrupting her thoughts,

Drew's words came out fast but quiet.

"Sure."

He started to open his mouth, but her bobber dipped under the water, and a tug pulled at her line. She whooped. "I think I got one!"

She released the tension then started to reel in her fish. When it was almost out of the water, she grabbed her line and lifted up the small bluegill. She laughed at the little thing that couldn't have weighed more than a pound. "Definitely not a keeper."

"But it's a fish."

"You're right about that, and who'd have thought I'd catch one at this time of day and in this heat?"

She bit her bottom lip to shut her mouth when Drew gawked at her. A knowing expression marked his face. "So you did know we probably wouldn't catch many."

She shrugged. "I'm a country girl, Drew. I've been fishing all my life."

Drew's laugh filled the air around them. His muscles seemed to loosen, and he relaxed. "I need to apologize to you, Melody."

His tone was somber and serious, and Melody knew he meant every word he said. She sat still, peering down at the cooler. She just couldn't seem to look him in the eye.

He continued. "My pride got the best of me. I don't have to tell you that I'm very competitive by nature."

A quick giggle slipped through her lips, and she pursed them shut. Sneaking a peek up at him, she saw that he was grinning at her. She gazed back down, but he put his thumb under her chin and lifted her face until her gaze met his. "You accepting Christ is the best thing I've heard in a long time. I want you to know that even though I was acting like a jerk, I had been praying for you almost nonstop."

Melody's heart pounded in her chest. She wasn't surprised. All along she knew which buttons to push on Drew Wilson to incite his competitive fury. He'd been the best competitor she'd ever challenged, and she'd fully enjoyed most of their battles.

"Drew, I wasn't innocent. I knew how to make you mad, and I enjoyed seeing you get angry. I'm sorry, too." She placed more bait on the hook. "As far as me being a Christian," she said as she cast out her line once more, "it is the best thing that's ever happened to me."

She shifted in her chair so that she was sitting on her left foot. "I can't stop reading my Bible. It's the funniest thing, because I hate reading. I've started with John because that's where Aunt Renee told me to start."

"Where are you in John?"

"Oh, I've finished it. I'm in Acts now." She pointed to her rod. "But isn't it interesting that Jesus was all about the fishing, and here we sit—fishing."

Drew chuckled. "You're right."

"I don't know why it took me so long to give my heart to Jesus." She cocked her head. "Actually, yes I do. I have a really hard time giving up control of anything, and that would include my life."

Her bobber dipped under the water again. She pulled back against the tug on her line. "I've got another one." Reeling in again, this time she pulled in a much larger bass. Grabbing its bottom lip with her left hand, she yanked out the hook with her right. "Look at that!"

Drew lifted his eyebrows. "Now, that's a keeper."

"It sure is." She waited while Drew opened the cooler so that she could place the fish inside.

"We'll have to have a cookout with the fish we catch."

She studied Drew for a moment. Once they'd said their piece, she was really having a good time with him. "That would be great." She bit her bottom lip. The urge to tease him welled inside her until she simply couldn't hold back. She elbowed his arm and winked. "You *have* realized I've got two fish to your none."

Drew leaned back and howled. "Yes, you have. And Melody Markwell"—he reached over and pinched her cheek as if she were a little child— "tonight I might just let you catch them all."

"Oh you *might*, huh? You want to make a bet?"

eleven

Drew was absolutely, one hundred percent, over-the-top smitten. Melody Markwell was everything he never realized he wanted in a woman. She was naturally beautiful. He remembered how gorgeous her amazingly long and silky brown hair looked blowing in the wind while they were fishing. Even pulled back in a ponytail, it was gorgeous.

And her eyes. Deep, dark brown. They were filled with such intensity and depth. So much truth. And when she teased him about her catching more fish, they had sparkled with delight. He could stare into those depths all day if she'd let him.

And her lips. Well, her lips were just downright difficult for him to be around. Thick and almost pouty, he had to stop himself from kissing her on more than one occasion the other night.

But more than her perfectly sun-kissed skin and her tiny frame, he was falling for who she was. Her inner strength drew him, as did her competitive nature. They'd always have fun battling over one thing or another.

But now with her zeal to know more about Christ and her honesty about what she understood and felt and thought, she inspired him to be a better Christian. She encouraged him to learn and study God's Word more.

I'm falling for her, God.

There was no use denying it or trying to dissuade it.

He didn't want to push it away. He'd spent too much time worrying about pride and winning. He didn't want to waste another moment on any of that.

Needing to talk with his friend, he'd driven to Mike's house. He knocked on the front door. Joe, Mike's little brother, answered it. The teen wasn't so little anymore. He was nearly as tall as Drew and as broad as his big brother, which didn't say a whole lot, as Mike was quite a bit smaller than him or Nick or even Wyatt. Still, the kid had grown up a lot.

"Hey, Drew." Joe grabbed Drew's hand in a firm handshake.

Drew was surprised at how strong Joe had become. If he remembered right, the boy was going into high school this year. He was probably a great help on the farm now. But then Drew wondered why the kid was standing in the door barefoot in shorts and a T-shirt. He obviously wasn't helping Mike and his dad at that moment. "I'm looking for your brother. You know where he is?"

He pointed around the back of the house. "In the back with Dixie."

"She have her pups?"

Joe nodded, but he turned his head toward the baseball game that was on the television.

Now that Drew came to think of it, the reason he'd been surprised at how much Joe had grown was because he hadn't seen Joe at church in a while. He frowned as he wondered what could be going on. He knew Joe played for a traveling baseball team that took him away from church some Sundays, but it had been quite a few weeks since Drew remembered seeing him. Drew waved. "Okay. Thanks."

Joe didn't respond. He simply shut the door, and Drew walked around the house and toward the shed. He spied Mike leaned up against the door, one leg crossed in front of the other. He was such a softy when it came to the animals having their babies. Mike was a good balance to him and Nick and Wyatt. Not the strongest in any physical way, Mike was the one with a good head and a tender heart.

"Hey, Mike."

Mike turned and put his finger up to his mouth. "Not too loud, man. You'll make Dixie nervous. She just settled in to nurse her brood."

Drew peeked in the shed door and saw the dark lab with several babies fighting for their spot to feed. Dixie saw him and let out a low growl.

Drew lifted his hands. "I'll move, Dixie girl. Don't get mad."

Mike pulled the shed door closed then looked at Drew. "She's just a little protective of her pups."

"How many did she have?"

"Six. Four boys and two girls." Mike studied him. "So what's up?"

"I need to talk to you about Lacy."

Mike rolled his eyes and blew out a breath. He walked away from Drew toward the barn. "I'm not talking to you about Lacy." He lifted his hand. "Just because you're dying to win that bet since Melody's been showing you up doesn't mean you need to hound me to ask that girl out on a date."

Mike's words stung, and part of Drew wanted to lay into him with both barrels. But he knew he couldn't fuss at Mike. His friend was right. Drew had been especially hard on Mike when it came to Lacy, and it probably had a lot to do with the fact that Melody kept kicking his tail every time they competed against one another. He'd been spending a lot of time learning to be on the losing side of the stick over the last few months.

"That's not exactly why I'm here." Drew shifted his feet. "Actually, it *is* sort of why I'm here."

Mike lifted his eyebrows and crossed his arms in front of his chest.

Drew spread open his arms. "Look, man, I've fallen for Melody. I'm crazy about the girl. I came over here to tell you to ask out Lacy anytime you want. I'm throwing in the towel and going after Melody. You win. I lose."

Mike furrowed his eyebrows and stared at Drew for a moment. Then he smiled and punched Drew in the shoulder. "It's about time you came to your senses. That girl is perfect for you."

Drew sucked in his breath at the thought of asking Melody to go on a date, on a real date with him. It made him nervous as the worm being baited on the hook, but Mike was right. She was perfect for him.

"I know." Drew extended his hand to Mike. "I can't stay. I just wanted to let you know I'm out. You win."

As he walked back to his truck, he imagined talking to her, fighting with her, kissing her soft lips. And now, he could worship with her. *God, a year ago I would have laughed if someone had said I'd want this, but Melody has changed my mind and my heart.*

The wheels in Drew's mind churned as he tried to think of the best way to tell her how he felt. As much fun as they'd had the other night fishing, he was sure she'd give him a chance. Still, he'd never asked a girl out before, and

Melody was special. He had to do it right.

❧

Since the day they'd planted it, Melody realized she loved working in her aunt's garden. She pulled another weed from the cucumber row she had planted almost two months before. Just as her aunt said, the plants had grown big and sprawled out along the ground. She had to pick up and dig around stems and leaves to find all the weeds.

She thought about how she had dug huge craters and nearly buried the poor things. So much had changed since that day. Drew and Addy returned home from their honeymoon. Uncle Roy had a stroke and amazingly was almost fully recovered. Baby Wyatt had gotten two teeth. She'd accepted Jesus.

Her heart swelled. It was the best, most exciting change she'd ever experienced. She still didn't understand a lot of things, and Aunt Renee warned her that God's Word promised she'd still have a bunch of problems to deal with and the world would still have a lot of bad things happen in it, but she felt such peace. She prayed God would give her faith no matter what happened in the future.

Finished pulling the weeds, she stood up, wiped her hands on her blue jean shorts, then grabbed her Bible off the back deck table. She walked along the small stone path her aunt had built. It led to a good-sized flower garden that surrounded a large shade tree. She sat down on the bench and watched as a small cardinal flew up above her and perched on a branch.

God's creation amazed her. With a slight sigh she picked up her Bible and opened to where she had a bookmark. She'd been reading about these two guys, Paul and

Barnabas, who were traveling all over the place telling people about Jesus. She didn't understand all of it, but apparently some of the believers who were Jews didn't like the idea of "other" people being able to accept Christ.

The thought baffled her a little bit. Aunt Renee tried to explain that she'd have to study the culture of the time, and how different groups of people didn't associate with each other. She just didn't quite understand why some of them wouldn't want everyone on the planet to be able to accept Jesus.

She wanted to tell the whole world about Him. She'd probably driven Gracie crazy talking about all she was learning about Jesus. She smiled at the thought. *It would serve her right for all those days she drove me nuts talking about God.*

More than anything, she wanted her mom to know Jesus. She still hadn't called Melody back. It stung, and a part of her wanted to wash her hands of her mother. But when she thought of how much she'd changed since accepting the Lord, she couldn't help but want the same thing for her mom.

She shifted to get more comfortable on the bench. She'd really liked the part in Acts where the guy—if she remembered right, it was Paul—talked about how after he'd stopped persecuting Jesus and accepted Him, this other guy came along and touched him, and then something that looked like scales fell off Paul's eyes. Then he could see, and he went to tell everyone about Jesus.

Melody had instantly felt a connection with that man, Paul. Not only did scales fall off her eyes so that she could see that she needed Jesus, but now she could also read His Word. It wasn't as if she couldn't read at all. She'd learned the basics, and she'd been forced to sit through plenty of "special" classes in school to help her along. But she just couldn't read very well.

Since she fell in love with Jesus, she couldn't seem to put her Bible down. She read it all the time. She didn't understand everything, and she had to ask a lot of questions of Aunt Renee and Gracie, but she was starting to get it. A lot of things were beginning to make sense.

She peered down at her Bible and began to read again. The two guys she'd been reading about, Paul and Barnabas, had a disagreement and decided to go their own ways. It made her a little sad, and she wondered why Paul didn't want to give Mark a second chance. Evidently, he'd skipped out on them when the pressure got hot in another town.

"Hey, you mind if I interrupt you for a second?"

Melody gazed up at Drew. He was already enormous compared to her, but with her sitting on a bench and him standing, he really towered over her.

She patted the empty side of the bench. "Only if you have a seat. I'll strain my neck trying to look up at you."

Drew chuckled, and she noticed that his neck and cheeks turned red when he sat beside her. She also realized he smelled pretty good, like a light, woodsy cologne. And he'd gotten a haircut. She could see a white line along his neck where his hair had guarded it from the sun.

He cleared his throat and leaned forward, placing his elbows on his knees. He clasped and unclasped his hands. Why was he so nervous? His acting that way was making her feel squeamish.

He finally spoke. "So have you enjoyed vacation Bible school?"

She sat up. "It has been a complete blast. Those senior ladies in the kitchen are a hoot. I was a little nervous when Audrey asked me to help out in the kitchen." She elbowed his arm. "We both know I'm not the best cook."

He chuckled.

"But those women have been so kind to me, and they've all promised to teach me how to 'find my way around the kitchen' as they put it."

Drew swiped one hand through his hair. He gazed out over her uncle's fields then looked back at her then back at his hands. "They're all wonderful. That's for sure."

She continued, "And Addy is amazing with music. Every chance I got I'd sneak a peek in the auditorium. She had those kids jumping and dancing and singing and shouting. Part of me wanted to just run right in there and join them."

"You should have."

Melody ducked her head. "I did." She giggled and held up two fingers. "Twice."

He smiled at her, but he didn't respond. Instead, he cleared his throat again, and Melody couldn't help but wonder if he'd come down with a cold or if he had a sore throat or something. "Have you got a cold? Do you want me to get you a drink?"

Bright red patches covered his neck and cheeks again, and Drew shook his head. "I was just wondering." He leaned back against the bench and wiped his hands on the front of his jeans. "Well, the Bible school picnic is Sunday evening. And I wondered if you'd want to go with me."

Melody shrugged. She didn't see any harm in that. She and Drew were friends now. Of course she'd be willing to go with him to the picnic. They were having cornhole and horseshoes and volleyball. She chuckled inwardly. She'd be his best competition. She may have given her heart to Jesus, but she was still going to whip up on Drew every chance she could. "Sure. Everyone will be there. It sounds like fun." She teasingly punched his arm. "I'll need a friend to whip at cornhole."

His expression fell as he stood up. A hesitant smile bowed his lips. "Great." He smacked the side of his leg. "I'll pick you at five."

Melody frowned as she watched Drew walk away. That was weird. She'd never seen Drew act that way.

❧

She didn't get it, Lord. She didn't understand that I was asking her on a date.

Drew leaned back against the seat in his truck. He smacked the top of the steering wheel then turned the ignition. The truck grumbled to life a little slower than she normally did. Ignoring it, he shifted her into REVERSE and pulled out of the driveway.

I wanted it to be perfect. When I saw her sitting under that tree reading her Bible, well, I thought there wasn't a better place in the world to ask her on our first date. But she thought I was just asking her to ride to the church with me—as a friend.

He stared out over the countryside as he made his way back to the homesite. He'd left his dad alone working on the electric because he wanted to ask her in person. And he had asked her. And she had said yes. But a lot of good that did. They were going as friends.

He pulled into what would soon be his driveway and turned off the truck. His dad walked out of the house and wiped sweat from his forehead. It was an awfully hot day in

July, and wiring a house sure didn't cool a fellow off. "How'd it go, son?"

"She said yes." Drew walked past his dad and back into the house.

"That's great." His dad followed behind him. "So why are you upset?"

"She thinks we're going as friends. It was obvious she didn't understand I was asking her on a date."

His dad laughed as he grabbed a water bottle out of the cooler. He wiped the outside of it against his forehead before he unscrewed the top and gulped a long drink. "Maybe that's for the best."

"What?"

His dad lifted his hands in surrender. "At least for right now. The girl's only just accepted Christ, and the two of you were at each other's throats just before that. Dating you might be a bit more than she can think about right now."

Drew chewed on his dad's words. He might be right. But at the same time, Drew didn't wait for anything. He wasn't one to sit on something and stew about it. If he wanted it, he went out and got it. He tried to follow the Lord's leading, and there were times he had to take things a little slower, but for the most part he just set his mind to something and went after it.

"I don't know, Dad. I just think I botched up asking her out. You know I'd never done it before."

"Let me ask you something, son. Is going to a church picnic really going on a date?"

Drew lifted his eyebrows and shrugged. "I don't know. It's somewhere I wanted to go with her."

"When you take a woman on a date, you want it to

be somewhere that you can get to know each other. Somewhere where everyone you know in the world isn't going to be there. Do you get what I'm saying?"

"So asking her to the picnic wasn't really like asking her on a date?" Drew pursed his lips. "You could have told me that to begin with."

A low chuckle escaped his dad's mouth as he shrugged. "Maybe so, but I thought you might want to figure it out on your own. That's how you usually like to do things."

Drew wrinkled his nose at him. His dad didn't have to point out that Drew was mule headed. He knew it all too well.

Merriment still lit his dad's eyes as he swatted Drew's arm. "Come on, son. Right now I need you to help me get this wire through the wall."

Drew helped his dad as his mind replayed his invitation to Melody. She talked with such ease with him now. The transformation had been so dramatic and sudden. He knew she still had her spunky, competitive spirit, and he loved that, too.

He'd just wait until they were at the picnic, and then he'd ask her again. This time he'd make sure she understood he wanted to take her on a date. Especially now that he understood taking her to a Bible school picnic wasn't a real one anyway.

twelve

Melody waited in line to load up her plate with several homemade foods at the Bible school picnic. Standing behind her, Drew pointed to tiny pieces of bread with some kind of dressing and cucumbers on top. "See those? Nelli Jo makes them. They're delicious."

Melody grabbed one and placed it on her plate. She'd never been to a potluck picnic of this sort until she'd come to visit her aunt and uncle. Most everything she and her mother ate came from a box or can.

He pointed to another dish. "There's Mom's potato salad."

Her mouth watered as she put a spoonful of Drew's mom's potato salad on her plate.

As they made their way down the line, she looked back at Drew's plate. It was already piled up with food, and they hadn't yet made it to the coleslaw. She wasn't going to tell Drew until after he'd tasted it, but she'd made it again. Only this time, Aunt Renee helped her with each step, and she hadn't forgotten the sugar.

"Oh yum." He pushed some of his food toward the middle of the plate with his fork. "I have to make room for Renee's coleslaw."

He scooped up a big spoonful and dropped it on his plate, then peered at Melody. A blush spread across his cheeks, and he started to open his mouth. She looked away from him, knowing he was probably remembering the last time he thought he was eating Aunt Renee's dish. *Well, this time he won't be disappointed.*

With her plate as full as she could get it, she walked over to the folding chair Drew brought for her and sat down. Though it was hot for late afternoon in July, the enormous shade tree they sat under kept it from being unbearable—as long as the insects left them alone. She swatted at a fly.

Drew joined her and set his plate in his chair. "I'm going to go get a drink. What would you like?"

"Sweet tea, of course."

He winked. "Of course."

He made his way to the table set up with several two-liter bottles of sodas as well as pitchers of lemonade and sweet tea. She noticed how strong he looked in the maroon T-shirt that hugged his true-farming-boy's muscles. As always, he wore jeans and boots. She wasn't sure she'd ever seen him without them. The white line along the edges of his haircut was now a bright red, sunburned from the hours he spent outside.

Drew was a good man. A hard worker. He was God-fearing. And he wasn't hard to look at either. *He'd make such a good husband.* Her face warmed at the thought.

He turned back around with two cups in his hands and made his way toward her. She averted her gaze even though she knew he didn't know what she was thinking. She didn't have those kinds of silly notions floating around in her mind. She knew all kinds of girls who dreamed of the boy they'd one day meet and marry. She didn't have those dreams. Hers were always about getting away.

Taking a bite of her food, she tried to shoo the thought

away. She wanted to feel normal in front of Drew, to enjoy their friendship.

"Mmm. Renee, the coleslaw is wonderful."

She looked up, and Drew had lifted his empty fork in the air at her aunt, who sat on the other side of him.

"Melody made it." Her aunt nonchalantly nodded toward her then continued to talk to the woman sitting beside her.

Drew turned to her. His eyebrows raised in surprise. He nodded. His eyes gleamed with just a hint of mischievousness. "Good job."

She placed her hand against her chest and batted her eyes, feigning arrogance. "Did you doubt I could do it?"

He blinked and cocked his head to one side. "Yes."

Melody swatted his arm for his teasing, and Drew laughed outright. "You gonna play me at cornhole?"

"Absolutely." He leaned close to her. "Now that you're a Christian, you gonna let me win?"

She wrinkled her nose. "Absolutely not."

He made a fist and gently tapped her jaw then pulled her ponytail. "That's my girl."

Melody's jaw dropped. "What are we? In seventh grade?"

Drew pinched her nose. "I happened to like seventh grade."

"Well then, I'll do you like I did every other thirteen-year-old boy when I was in middle school."

In one quick motion, she dropped her plate to the ground, jumped up, moved behind Drew, and wrapped her arm around his neck in a headlock. She rubbed his head with the knuckles of her free hand and yelled, "You want a piece of me, big guy? You think you can mess with me?"

Laughing, Drew hopped up to his full height, but Melody didn't let go even though her feet were dangling in the air. Reaching around his back with one arm, he grabbed her around the waist and twisted her until she was in front of him.

For a moment, panic set in as she realized Drew was so much bigger and stronger than she was. They were only playing, but fear flooded her for a brief moment. He must have seen it in her eyes because hc let her go.

Knowing she shouldn't be afraid, she tried to laugh as she lifted her hands up. "You got me."

She looked around, noting how many of their church friends were covering their mouths and giggling at their antics. Uncle Roy even appeared downright amused. She pointed at Drew and tried to chuckle. "He got me there. Beat me that time."

Drew had already sat back down. He gazed at her with too much intensity. He was trying to read what had happened. God was working on her heart, teaching her to trust. She just wished she could completely get over her past.

❧

Drew's hands wouldn't stop sweating as he drove Melody back to Roy and Renee's place. He'd been puzzled about her reaction to their horseplay before the kids performed their Bible school program. He thought he saw fear in her gaze, but that didn't make sense. He'd never given her any reason to be afraid of him. The only thing he could figure was that she got embarrassed teasing around like that in front of the whole church.

He liked that she'd gotten so spunky with him. She didn't back down for anything, even though she probably didn't weigh a hundred pounds soaking wet. He snuck a quick peek at her in the passenger's seat.

She was tired. It had been an eventful couple of weeks for her. If he knew her well at all, he figured she'd spent plenty an evening staying awake far too long trying to soak in more of what the Bible said. Then she'd have to get up early to head over to AJ's for work. He loved that she was so excited, but a girl needed her rest.

Several times she'd started to lay her head back, but he'd hit a pothole, and she'd wake back up. He tried to be careful, but there wasn't much a man could do with these old country roads and his pickup.

He huffed. Here he had been so mad that she didn't understand he was trying to ask her on a date to the church picnic. His dad had been right. That wasn't no kind of date. A date would be just the two of them going to dinner or seeing a movie or whatever it was people liked to do. His idea of a perfect date would be going fishing and then frying up the catch, but he probably wouldn't mind eating dinner somewhere nice either.

His heartbeat sped up as he got closer to the house. He was determined to ask her. In fact, he'd made up his mind that he would not pull out of Roy's driveway until he had.

Trying to get up his nerve, he slowed the truck just a bit. No sense in getting there any faster than he already was. His stomach started to churn. *Please, God. Help me through this. I've helped cows birth their calves, killed more copperheads than I can count, but the thought of asking this woman on a date absolutely terrifies me.*

Unable to go any slower, he finally had no choice but to pull into the driveway. Melody smiled at him as she reached for the door. "Thanks for the ride, Drew. It was fun."

She turned the handle, and Drew thought he might be sick at any moment. She couldn't leave. He had to ask her on a date. He reached across her and pulled the door shut. She gawked at him in surprise. A mixture of anger and panic flashed across her face. He sat back in his seat. "Wait a minute, Melody. I want to ask you something."

She stared at him, and for a moment Drew wondered if reaching over her like that had been a bad idea. He couldn't think that through right now though. He had to get up the nerve to just spit it out.

"Okay?" Melody's tone was sarcastic, and he knew he needed to say it and quick.

Grabbing the steering wheel, he gripped it with all his might. "I was wondering if you'd like to have dinner with me sometime."

He blew out a long breath. There, he'd said it. He'd finally gotten the nerve to ask her out. Now he only needed to hear her say yes. He looked at her, but he couldn't read the expression on her face.

"I'm sorry, Drew. I can't."

Before he could respond, she opened the door, stepped out, and raced into the house.

੩

Melody lowered into Gracie's oversized leather recliner and nestled Wyatt close to her chest to feed him his milk. Already a little grumpy and ready for his afternoon nap,

Wyatt whimpered and reached for the bottle. She stuck it in his mouth, and he closed his eyes and gulped it down. "I still can't believe Drew asked me out."

She rocked the chair, and Wyatt reached up and grabbed a strand of her hair and twisted it around his hand. In a matter of moments he would be fast asleep.

"I'm not surprised." Gracie popped a chocolate-covered peanut into her mouth. "It was obvious he was falling for you."

"How so? All we ever did was fight."

"That was how we knew." She popped another peanut. She pointed to the almost-empty plastic container. "You know this is why I'm still not losing my baby weight."

Melody grinned. "How would us fighting make you know he liked me?"

Gracie gave her an exasperated look. "Do you know how many girls have hit on Drew Wilson over the years?"

A niggling of jealousy crept up Melody's spine. Just how many women had liked Drew, and why did it bother her that they had? She looked down at Wyatt. His bottle was already almost gone, and he'd fallen asleep. She gently lifted him up to her shoulder and patted his back. "No. I guess I don't."

Gracie flipped her hand. "Let me tell you, there have been plenty, but he's never given any of them the time of day. Until you."

Wyatt burped, waking himself. She continued to pat his back, and he snuggled into her shoulder until he had fallen asleep again. "I never chased after him."

"I know."

"So, why?"

"Melody, you've always been a terrific person, and you're beautiful, even if you do try to hide it behind a ponytail." Gracie popped another chocolate-covered peanut in her mouth then waved her arms in the air. "And now that you're a Christian, you are simply a–mazing."

Melody bit her bottom lip and grinned at Gracie's dramatics. She sobered and closed her eyes. "I can't go on a date with him."

"Why?"

Melody took a long breath. She wasn't sure she wanted to tell Gracie.

thirteen

Drew spent the last several days trying to get over Melody's rejection. He'd wanted nothing to do with women before her, so he should be able to just move on with life as normal. Yet he couldn't get her out of his mind.

He'd tried putting all his effort and energy into the house, and he'd gotten a lot accomplished, but he'd also had to redo things because he couldn't concentrate properly. Most of the plumbing and electrical work was finished except for the more cosmetic things.

About to install the kitchen sink, he moved a few scrap boards and stray nails in search of the supplies he needed. He hollered into the other room, "Nick, have you seen a marker?"

Nick walked into the kitchen holding a black one in his hand. "Looking for this?"

"Yep." He pointed to the template he'd already taped in place on the counter. "Just need to mark this, and I can cut my hole."

Drew outlined the template then picked up the drill, ready to drill holes in each corner. He was getting kind of hungry, as he and Nick had been working for quite a while, but he figured he could at least get the hole cut into the countertop.

"Hang on, man." Nick lifted his hand to stop him. "Look, it's a bit off center."

"No way." Drew inspected his markings. They did seem a bit off, but he'd measured twice before he'd taped down the template. Exasperated, he pulled out a tape measure and measured both sides. Sure enough, Nick was right. He'd almost drilled holes a full three-eighths of an inch off center. He placed his hands on the counter and ducked his head. "I don't know what's wrong with me."

"I've got a hunch."

Drew turned around and leaned his backside against the counter. He crossed his arms in front of his chest. He'd worked so hard on this house. Didn't owe a penny for it, and lately, he'd been wasting a lot of pennies with little mess ups like the one Nick just prevented. "Your hunch is probably right."

Nick grabbed the cleaning spray and a paper towel off the floor. He sprayed the counter then wiped off the marker. "Don't give up on her. She just needs some time."

Drew scoffed as he pointed at his own chest. "Me? Give up? When have you ever known me to give up on anything?"

Nick threw the towel at Drew's chest. "Never. And that was what I wanted to hear."

Drew didn't want to give up on her, but his pride stung a bit, too. Part of him couldn't stop thinking about her, day and night. That part told him to just keep praying and that when the time was right she'd want to go on a date with him. The other part of him wanted to throw in the towel, to somehow get her out of his mind for good.

He glanced at his watch. "It's getting pretty close to lunchtime. I think I'm going to take a break."

"Yeah. I've got to go. I promised Addy I'd come home for lunch."

Just as Drew figured, his sister, Addy, had his best friend on a tight schedule. Nick used to do what he wanted when he wanted. Now he always had to do things with Addy. He never thought the day would come, but Drew wanted that with Melody.

They left the house and got into their trucks. Drew stuck his arm out the window. "Thanks for the help. See you later."

Nick nodded then drove off. Drew made his way into town. He planned to grab a bite of some real food at the diner before he headed back to work on the kitchen sink again. Maybe a little protein would help his overworked mind to focus better.

He passed AJ's shop, and it felt as if a knife twisted in his gut. She was there. He was sure of it. AJ had been as tickled as a boy who got his first bike on Christmas ever since Melody started working for him. From what Drew heard, they could hardly handle all the work she'd brought in. AJ had even hired another worker to do nothing but oil changes.

He pulled into the diner's parking lot. It would be so easy to just walk over there and talk to her. They were friends, and there wouldn't be anything wrong with him saying hello to a friend. He envisioned her rejection and how she didn't even look back to say good-bye as she rushed into Roy and Renee's house.

He was probably the last person she wanted to see. But he cared about her, and he wasn't a quitter. He couldn't just give up on his feelings without at least finding out why she'd dismissed him so quickly.

Fighting the urge to walk over to the shop, he made his way into the diner. Mike had a lot to do on the farm today and wouldn't be meeting Drew for lunch. Wyatt and Nick rarely ate with them anymore, now that they were married. But Drew didn't mind being alone today. He was tired of thinking, but he really didn't want to do any talking or explaining either.

The place was unusually busy, so Lacy simply took his order, brought out his food, and left him alone. He was glad for that. The meat loaf was good. It was always good. But it didn't do much for the ache that just wouldn't leave his gut.

God, I can't stand this. I have to try again. At least get her to tell me why she doesn't want to go on a date with me.

Before he could change his mind, Drew paid the bill and walked straight to AJ's. He saw the most adorable, coverall-covered, female legs stuck out from beneath a truck. Not wanting to startle her, he waited until she'd slid herself out from under it. Her eyebrows lifted in surprise when she saw him.

"Hello, Melody."

She sat up and pulled a cloth from her front pocket. She started to wipe her hands, and Drew thought by the sparkle that seemed to light her eyes that she was happy to see him. "Hi, Drew."

"I need to ask you a favor."

She averted her gaze but still nodded. "Okay."

His mind raced trying to think of something he needed her help with. He couldn't come up with anything, but he had to have some reason, some favor to ask of her. He needed the chance to talk to her. "I need you to come look at my tractor."

She looked back at him with an unconvinced expression across her face. She opened her mouth to say something then shut it. Smiling at him, she nodded her head again. "Okay. I'll come by after work."

Drew's spirits lifted. She was going to stop by his house. He was going to have the opportunity to talk to her again.

He waved and almost tripped over his own feet as he walked out of the garage. The only problem was there was nothing wrong with his tractor. A twinge of guilt tickled his conscience, and he knew he was going to have to head out there and pull a belt off that tractor.

❧

Melody was going to tell Drew the truth. She prayed for guidance as she drove out to his house. It seemed like forever since she'd been there. She remembered how much fun they'd had fishing together. He'd been so cute when he apologized for the way he acted at the tractor pull, and she knew he had been sincere.

It had been several weeks since she drove through the thick patch of trees. She gasped when she reached the clearing. The house! It looked like a house. And he'd made it a log cabin. It had a porch that extended the full length of the front. Surely he'd have a deck on the back. It only made sense.

Wondering what it looked like inside, she knew she wouldn't be able to ask Drew about it. For a moment, she imagined a dark brown leather couch and love seat around a stone fireplace. She'd seen the coolest lamps with stick bundles as pedestals that would look perfect in a log home. She loved deep red accents, and she knew the color would look perfect as part of the rug and possibly in a few pictures in the home Drew had built. *What am I thinking? Why am I decorating his house in my mind?*

She shook the thoughts away. She didn't know what he would think of her once she told him everything. She should just get over her past. She'd put her trust in God, and Drew would probably think she should no longer have this fear of losing control. But a girl didn't change something that had gripped her for so long overnight. God was working on her heart, but she wasn't ready to date.

Drew already stood beside the tractor he needed her to look at. She grinned. She knew he didn't need her to look at it. The man knew how to fix a broken belt. *If it's even broken.*

After parking the truck, she hopped out and walked over to him. Before she could say hello, he handed a belt to her. "I can't lie to you. I took it off to get you to come out here."

Despite her nervousness, Melody laughed outright. She grabbed the belt from his hands. "Thanks for the honesty. Now you get to help me put it back on."

"Not a problem." They worked together, and in no time the belt was back on the tractor, and it was running as it should.

He handed her a rag to wipe off her hands. "Melody, I have to just be honest with you. I'm really attracted to you. I think you're something special. I'd really like you to give me a chance."

Melody closed her eyes. Unlike most girls, she hadn't

dreamed of this moment. She didn't seek out attention from boys. She tried to avoid them, tried to beat them at every game they played.

But she did like Drew. She was drawn to him as she'd never been drawn to a man before. There were moments when she could lose herself in visions of dating him. Then she'd think about her reaction to their playing at the church Bible school picnic. She didn't want to have that kind of response to her boyfriend, one of fear because he was bigger and stronger than she was. Drew didn't deserve that.

No. She wasn't ready to date. Not Drew. Not anyone. She peered up into his beautiful eyes and shook her head. "I can't."

He placed his hand against the tractor. "Why not? I know I wasn't the best witness to you. I've come to realize it's because I was so intrigued by you that I acted as I did. I know you've been interested in me. I've seen it in your eyes."

Melody sighed. Her heart pounded beneath her chest. She didn't want to tell him what happened. She'd never really shared it out loud, except with her mom on the day it happened. She couldn't even make herself share it with Gracie the other day. Besides, her fear went deeper than her attacker. It was also a lack of trust in men because of her dad.

"It's really not you."

He huffed and looked away from her.

She continued. "I know that's just a saying, but it's the truth." She paused, blew out a breath, then said, "When I was fourteen, I was trying out for the cross-country team. I loved that I could run and take my mind off my stresses at home. So I went for a jog in the park. It was early, and no one was really out...."

She stopped and swallowed the knot in her throat. Her hands started to tremble, and she shoved them into her coverall pockets.

Drew peered down at her. Concern etched his face. "What happened?"

She felt tears pooling in her eyes. The words were hard to say out loud. They were embarrassing, humbling. If she hadn't been out so early, she would have never been confronted. She swiped her eyes with the back of her hand and lifted her chin. She was determined to tell him the truth.

"I was jogging, and a man grabbed me. I didn't know where he came from. He was just there." She touched her arm where his hand had gripped her. "And he was stronger than me. He threw me on the ground."

"Did he rape you?" Drew's voice was low, and his expression was serious. He looked like a bear about to protect his cub. She knew he wanted to find the man who'd hurt her, and in truth his reaction warmed her heart.

She shook her head. "Praise God, no. A woman pushing her baby in a stroller happened by and scared him away. But now, I still get afraid. I still—"

"That was the look you gave me when we were playing at the picnic. I couldn't figure out why you had fear in your eyes."

"You see, I shouldn't have. You haven't done anything to scare me, and yet I had a moment of panic because you are so much bigger and stronger than I am."

Slowly he reached up and touched her cheek with the back of his hand. She willed herself not to flinch then relished the feel of his warm skin on hers. He wouldn't hurt her. He would protect her. "Melody, I would never hurt you."

"I know." She pulled his hand away from her cheek. "But I'm not ready. I don't know if I'll ever be ready."

❧

Drew wanted to find the man who'd hurt Melody and rip him apart, limb by limb. Only a no-good coward would do such a thing to a woman. If he'd happened upon the scene that morning in the park, he'd have whipped that man's tail.

He sucked in a long breath and exhaled extra slow. He had to settle down. He couldn't change what happened to her. All he could do was show her how different he was than that disgusting man. He could be her friend. He could pray for her.

God, I know exactly what I can do for her.

Drew looked at Melody. The sun was starting to set. The pink and orange glow of the sky behind her made her look like a perfect character drawn in a picture. He'd seen that beautiful, long hair flowing down her shoulder only a few times, and now he longed to pull out that rubber band and watch it drop down to her waist. Every girl he knew caked makeup on her face. But not Melody, and she was still indescribably beautiful.

It will be hard for me not to want more from her.

His Spirit seemed to encourage Drew. *"I will give you strength."*

He started to reach out his hand to touch a stray strand of hair that brushed her cheek. Coming to his senses, he shoved his hand in his front pocket. "Tell you what. I still want to be friends."

Melody lifted her chin and gazed up at him. The vulnerability in her eyes was almost more than Drew could handle. "I'd really like that. I really want you to be my friend. I really do."

Drew bit back a grin at her emphatic reply. In his gut, he knew she did care for him. She probably wanted him to be more than a friend, and she needed him to be patient. *You know patience isn't my strong point, Lord.*

"You can do all things through Me."

He cleared his throat and went on with his idea. "How 'bout we meet out here a couple times a week for Bible study and maybe a little fishing." He pointed to the big old oak tree on the right side of the pond. "I'll set us up a bench or a table or something over there for our studying."

Melody's eyes lit up, and she clapped her hands. "Would you put up a swing? That branch is perfect for a. . ." Her face turned crimson, and she ducked her head and lifted her shoulders as if she'd just gotten caught doing something mischievous. "Sorry. I just think it'd be such a fun place to swing. It's perfect, and—"

Drew lifted his hand. "Consider it done." He pinched her nose. "And you'll be the first to swing on it."

She put up both her fists like she was going to box him. "You don't want me to put you in a headlock again."

Drew laughed and shook his head. "So, when do you want to start?"

Melody shrugged. "Tomorrow night?"

"Tomorrow night." Drew led her back to her truck

and opened the door for her. She seemed hesitant and embarrassed as she hopped inside. "I can hardly wait."

She leaned her arm out the window. "Thanks for being patient with me, Drew."

Drew wasn't sure what to say.

She started the truck and shifted it into gear but kept her foot on the brake. She peered out across the expanse of his property, seeming to drink in every intricate detail. "It's absolutely beautiful out here." She smiled at him then drove off.

He waved as he whispered, "One day you will share it with me."

fourteen

Melody was elated that she and Drew would be studying God's Word together. If there was a man in all the world that she wanted to help her overcome her fear and need for control at the feet of her Father, it would be Drew Wilson. Though it made little sense to her, she wanted to do something, to look prettier than she normally did when she went to Drew's later that evening.

She only had an hour for lunch, and Gracie wasn't expecting her today, but she raced to her house anyway. Melody didn't know exactly what she wanted Gracie to do, but surely the woman would have some ideas.

She knocked on the front door and within moments Gracie opened it. A full grin spread her lips. "Melody, it's so good to see you. Come on—"

Melody interrupted her friend and sped into the house. "I need your help."

Gracie furrowed her eyebrows as she shut the door. "Okay. Is something wrong?"

Wyatt squealed from inside his playpen and reached up to Melody. Unable to withstand any fussing from that precious boy, Melody scooped him up into her arms. He immediately reached for her hair. "Nothing's wrong. I've agreed to do Bible study with Drew, but just as friends."

"Okay?" Gracie still looked confused.

"And I want to do something about my hair."

"What's wrong with your hair? It's gorgeous."

Warmth trailed up her neck. "I mean, I don't want to wear it up in a ponytail, and I don't know what to do with it."

Gracie squinted and cocked her head. "I thought you were going to be just friends."

Melody huffed and shifted Wyatt to her other hip. "We are." She nestled her nose into the baby's neck, avoiding eye contact with her friend. "I just want to look a little prettier."

Gracie lifted her eyebrows and slowly nodded her head. "I see."

Melody rolled her eyes. "I'm not ready for Drew to be my boyfriend, but when I am ready—"

"You want Drew to be your boyfriend."

Embarrassed by the conversation as she simply hadn't considered falling for someone, Melody dug her face into Wyatt's chest. The boy squealed and grabbed her hair with both hands. She mumbled into his shirt. "Will you help me?"

Gracie laughed as she pried her boy off Melody's head. "Of course." Wyatt screamed and reached for Melody. "If my son will let me."

Melody walked to one of the straight-back dining room chairs and sat down. She reached for Wyatt again. "Here, I'll hold him in my lap. You fix my hair. But tell me what you're doing so I'll know how to do it."

"Sounds great."

Gracie left the room and within moments returned with a brush and a fat curling iron. Melody listened as Gracie talked about rolling the bottom of the back of her hair under and rolling the sides along her face. It felt nice to have someone fix her hair.

"Make sure whatever you're doing isn't hard to do, or I'll never do it."

Gracie snorted. "Melody, your hair is naturally amazing. I'm doing hardly anything at all."

To Melody's surprise only ten or fifteen minutes had passed when Gracie said she was done. She handed Wyatt to his mom and walked into the bathroom to see what she'd done. It was too hot, and her hair was too long to let all of it fall, so Gracie had pulled up the sides in one big clip at the top.

She'd left just a few curled strands touching each cheek. Slight curls flowed from the clip and all the way down her back. Some of them were shaped from the curler, but most were there naturally. Melody looked pretty, but not too different. She still felt like herself.

She bit her bottom lip and smiled when Gracie and Wyatt came into the bathroom and looked at her reflection as well. "It looks good, Gracie."

"You're such a natural beauty. What I wouldn't give for that hair." She lifted a curl in her hand then winked into the mirror. "Have fun with your friend."

"God's getting me there. I just know it."

☙

Drew had gotten up extra early to get his work done on the farm. It had been a challenge keeping up the farm and building his house, but God blessed him with extra strength the last few months. The fact he'd been unable to sleep several nights fretting over despising Melody or falling in love with her had also helped him.

This morning, he'd wanted to get a swing up on the tree as a surprise. He knew she wouldn't expect him to have it up so fast, but in order to do it, he'd had to make an unplanned trip to town to get what he needed. He'd also stopped by the diner to pick up a pitcher of their homemade sweet tea, as he knew she really liked it.

He set up two benches on the other side of the tree. He kept moving them so that they angled correctly away so that the sun didn't smack either one of them in the eye. Then he realized it would be near time for the sun to set once they met, so he arranged them again to be able to enjoy the sunset.

I feel like a girl fussing over my company coming over. He wrinkled his nose as he thought of the times his mom and sister had raced around the house, picking up blankets and moving pillows so that it looked nice before their guests arrived. He spread out his hands after he moved the bench one more time. *It's fine, Wilson,* he cajoled himself. *We're going to be focusing on God's Word, as friends.*

He heard a truck coming up the gravel road. He knew it was her. He took the Bible off the top of the cooler that held the sweet tea and placed it on one of the benches. Wringing his hands together, he knew it was ridiculous to be this nervous. His biggest concern was that he wouldn't be able to simply meet with her as a friend. *But I have no choice for now, God. Help me wait for Your timing.*

Melody parked beside his almost-finished house as Drew made his way around the pond toward her. She stepped out of the truck, and Drew gasped. That long, amazing, dark hair flowed freely all the way down her back except for a clip at the top of her head to hold up the sides.

She wasn't dressed up, but the blue jeans she wore looked like a mix between shorts and full-length jeans. They kinda hit just below her knees, but they looked really cute on her. Kinda feminine. And her top was a light pink. Pink! It was plain—no lace or frills like what Addy would wear—but it still looked very pretty on Melody. He swallowed hard, thankful he still had a little ways to walk to collect himself before he got to her.

Drew noted that she seemed to not know exactly what to do as he made his way to her. The breeze blew at her hair, and she just kinda kept swiping it away from her face with her fingers.

"Hey," he said when he reached her. "You look really pretty."

"Thanks." She stared out over the pond, and he noted the blush that spread along her neck. She glanced at him then looked away. "You got the swing up."

"Sure did, and you're going to try it out after our Bible study." He reached out and touched her arm. "Come on."

He let go of her right away so that she wouldn't feel uncomfortable then headed the way back to the tree. She sat down on one of the benches and placed her Bible in her lap, and Drew sat across from her. He noticed she'd also put on some pink paint on her lips. Not real dark. It looked pretty, but all these little things she'd done were going to make it doubly hard for him to concentrate on just being friends.

"I thought we'd start with one of the fishing stories in

the book of Matthew, if that's all right with you," Melody offered. She didn't look up from her Bible but focused on finding the right page. "Since we both love fishing and all."

"Sounds great to me. What chapter?"

"Fourteen." She twisted the cloth bookmark in her Bible around her index finger. "If you don't mind, I'll read it. I'm not a good reader, but I understand better when I'm the one reading."

"That's fine. You want me to pray first?"

"Okay."

Melody bowed her head. Drew wanted to reach over and take her hands in his, but he knew she might not be ready. He wasn't ready. If he touched her, he wouldn't be able to focus on the scriptures. He said a quick prayer to bless their time, the whole time praying in his heart that God would help him be a good friend.

When he'd finished, Melody looked up at him and smiled. She seemed more at ease as she started reading God's Word. Drew was surprised at how much she stumbled through the passage, but he had to give her credit that she never stopped. She'd fight to pronounce a word, conquer it, then go on to the next.

He thought of Melody's competitiveness and her need to be in control. Between a father who'd left her and her mother, a man who'd tried to rape her, and the struggles she'd obviously faced in school, Drew understood why Melody sought to be in charge of every area of her life. She'd been knocked down a lot, but she was a fighter and always determined to come out on top. *Now that You're the head of her life, God, she is already victorious.*

She finished reading, and they talked about Jesus feeding the multitude with only a few fish and loaves of bread. She marveled at the miracles Jesus performed. She put her index finger against her lips. "But did you notice what it says Jesus did?"

Drew shook his head.

She lifted her hands in the air and looked up at the sky. "He lifted the food up to God to bless it. Did He really have to do that? Wasn't Jesus able to do the miracle on His own? It seems to me that He could have, but He got God's blessing first." She lowered her voice and her hands. "He kind of gave it over to God."

Drew knew she was talking about control and trust and faith and handing all of it over to Jesus. He felt humbled by the innocence of her words. He wanted so much for Melody to date him. He prayed the *friendship* stage wouldn't last too long, but he'd been looking at it from the wrong perspective.

Anew, he inwardly took his feelings for Melody to the foot of the cross and laid them down. God knew when and if the time was right, and Drew would trust Him with it.

Once they finished their Bible study, Drew said a short prayer of thanksgiving for their time together. When he opened his eyes, Melody leaned forward on the bench and patted his hand. "Thanks, Drew." She raised one eyebrow as she glanced over at the swing then back at him. "Can I swing now?"

Drew laughed. "If I can push."

"*If* you can push. Buddy, I was gonna make you push." She hopped up from the bench and jumped onto the swing.

She bounced up and down a few times as she looked up at the branch. "You sure this can hold me?"

"Are you doubting my ability to tie knots, or are you suggesting I'd enjoy watching you fall on your tail?"

Melody pursed her lips and twisted her mouth. "Hmm. Both."

Drew moved behind her and grabbed both ropes above her head. "You're not going to fall, little lady."

He gave her a good push and she swung forward with a squeal. He continued to push, her from behind as she lifted her legs forward and backward, going as high as she could.

Her youthful spirit was like a balm to his tired soul. He'd been so wrapped up in competition and pride for so long that this woman, who could beat him at almost any sport she set out to challenge him at, made him sit back and smile. She was a lot of fun, and Drew had needed to learn not just to win, but to have fun. He was going to enjoy having her as a friend.

fifteen

A month had passed since Melody started having Bible studies with Drew. Her faith in God had grown so much as she learned about Paul's adventures in telling others about Christ. He'd endured so much pain and so many trials, but he never gave up on his faith.

But when Drew suggested they read about some of the women from the Old Testament, Melody had been more than intrigued by the strength and faith of Deborah, the judge who led the Israelite people to battle. She'd marveled in Ruth's faith to walk away from her people and all she knew, and Esther's courage to go before the king.

So many people—men *and* women—had endured all kinds of troubles and problems, and they'd stayed true to God. But what she loved more than anything was that God had stayed true to them. Not everything was easy. She'd read that with her own lips, but God had remained faithful. She could trust Him.

"Melody, will you go get a couple more cucumbers out of the garden?" Her aunt's voice sounded from the kitchen.

"Sure, Aunt Renee." Melody made her way out the back door. As they did at least two times a month, Drew's parents, Drew, and Addy and Nick were all coming over for dinner. Now that Roy had recovered, he enjoyed whipping up on everyone at the Wii tennis game. She was thankful he'd had a good report the last time he went to the doctor.

Addy and Nick pulled into the driveway as Melody walked back into the house with several cucumbers loading down her arms. Careful not to mess up her sundress, she dumped them in the sink to be washed then received a hug from her cousin and then from Addy.

Addy held her at arm's length. "I knew that dress would look pretty on you."

Melody smiled. "I'm glad you talked me into it."

Addy turned her around. "Bright colors look so good with your dark hair and eyes, and as dark as you've gotten this summer. . ." She swatted her hand through the air. "You needed some bright colors."

Melody glanced down at the plain bright yellow dress that had just a touch of embroidery at the bottom. "I really do like it."

Addy leaned close to her and whispered in her ear. "Drew will like it, too."

Melody felt as if a patch of butterflies fluttered through her heart. She and Drew had gotten to know each other so well over the last month. They'd fished together and played games together; she'd even helped him pick out some stuff for his house. Though she loved Addy and Gracie was her best girlfriend, Drew had truly become her best friend.

They'd prayed earnestly for her mother together, whom she'd only talked to one time in the last month and for only a few short minutes. They'd shared hopes and dreams. He'd even let it slip that he wanted as many children as God allowed. She hadn't admitted to him that she felt the same.

She finally felt ready to be more than friends with him.

Drew and his parents walked into the house. He smiled and winked at her as he pointed from his shoulders to his knees. He mouthed the words *I like your new dress.*

Addy leaned toward her and whispered, "Told ya."

Melody giggled as she walked toward Drew's mom and took a dish from her hands.

"Thanks, honey." She peered around the room. "Where's Renee?" She glanced back down at Melody and smiled. "By the way, I like your dress."

"I'm here." Renee walked out of the back room wiping her hands on a towel. "The hamburgers should be almost done. Is everyone hungry?"

Roy nudged Drew's dad's arm. "She's joking, right?"

He shrugged. "I suppose, because we're always hungry."

"Oh hush, you two." Aunt Renee swatted at them. "Give us a second to get spoons for all the dishes."

Melody hadn't realized Drew walked behind her until he touched her arm. With his other hand he crooked his finger, gesturing for her to follow him. They walked through the mudroom and out the back door.

He gently touched the side of her face with the back of his hand. Closing her eyes for just a moment, she thrilled at the touch, having not felt any fear with him in a long time. When she opened her eyes, he pressed a soft kiss on her forehead. "You are absolutely beautiful, Melody."

She bit her bottom lip, unsure how to respond.

"I brought you something." He pulled a small yellow daisy from behind his back. He stuck it behind her ear. "Matches your dress perfectly."

Melody giggled. "I can't wear this to dinner." She took it out from behind her ear and twirled the stem between her fingers. "But it was sweet of you."

"Come on, everybody. Let's eat." Her uncle Roy's anxious voice sounded from inside the dining room.

Melody wrinkled her nose. "We'd better get inside, or we're gonna get in trouble."

Drew motioned for her to go first. She walked back into the house. Yes, she was definitely ready to add more than friendship to her relationship with Drew.

❧

Drew was going to ask Melody on another date. He wouldn't do it today. They'd enjoy dinner with their families, probably play some cornhole, and Roy would whip all of them at tennis on the Wii. But their next Bible study session, he was going to ask her.

He'd already planned where they were going. There was a nice restaurant, right on the Kentucky River. It was a little ways from River Run, but he'd heard it was worth the drive. As soon as she accepted, he'd make reservations for them to have a sunset dinner on their patio. Seeing Melody in that beautiful yellow dress, he could hardly wait to take her on a date, just the two of them.

"Could you pass me some more of that potato salad?" Roy asked.

Drew handed him the bowl, but not before scooping a bit more out for himself.

"Hey now. No one said you could get some, too." Roy smiled at Drew. "I hear the house is almost done."

He swallowed his bite of food. "It is."

"When you going to have all of us for a cookout?"

He wiped his mouth. "Well, I'm still finishing the back deck."

"It looks really good, Uncle Roy," Melody added. Drew looked at her, and she grinned. He knew how much she loved the idea that he'd put a door on his bedroom that connected to the deck. One day, when she agreed to be his wife, she would be able to enjoy sitting on that deck, watching the sunrise in the mornings.

Drew agreed. "It does." He pointed to Melody. "And Melody's helped a lot."

"I haven't done much."

"Sure you have."

His dad smacked his hand down on the table. "When are you two lovebirds gonna quit going round and just decide you like each other?"

Drew watched as Melody's face washed bright crimson. His mom swatted his dad's arm. "Brian, that is up to them. You don't go blabbering out things like that."

Drew opened his mouth to say something. He didn't know what he would say, but anything to ease Melody's embarrassment. The phone rang before he could speak. Renee picked up the cordless phone from the hutch that sat behind her. A deep frown wrapped her face. "Oh no."

She stood and walked away from the table. Drew and everyone watched as she covered her mouth. "Oh no. How?"

The room grew quiet as an eerie feeling blanketed them. Something had happened. Drew tried not to let his mind wander with possibilities.

"Where is the family?" Renee's eyes filled with tears as

she raked the fingers of her free hand through her hair. "I'm so sorry. So very sorry. Yes, we're all together. I'll tell them."

She clicked the phone off and looked at the family. She cupped her hand over her mouth. Drew held his breath as he waited for her to talk. "There's been an accident."

Roy had already started to shake his head. "What happened, honey?"

"Mike's little brother, Joe. He was boating at the lake with some friends yesterday. The kids stayed out too late, swimming when it was too dark. They couldn't find him until this morning. He drowned."

❧

Melody felt like she was in a daze as she moved forward with Aunt Renee and Uncle Roy in line at the funeral home. She didn't know Mike's family very well, and of the three of Nick's good friends, Mike was the one she knew the least. Still, to have his little brother, only fourteen years old, die so suddenly. It was awful, and her heart broke for the family.

She waved to Drew, Nick, Addy, Wyatt, and Gracie, who all stood at the far corner of the room. Baby Wyatt wasn't with them. She assumed Gracie's mom was taking care of him.

They moved a few more steps forward. A large man still blocked her view of Mike, but she could see his mom and dad. Their faces were red and puffy from probably having cried for days. The man moved forward, and Melody saw the exhaustion and sadness that etched Mike's face. He had his arm around his mother's shoulders, and she knew he tried to be strong.

They moved forward again. Her aunt wrapped her

arms around Mike's mother. "I'm so sorry." She patted the woman's back. "So, so sorry."

Uncomfortable and unsure what to say, Melody simply mumbled her condolences and shook Mike's parents' hands. She reached Mike and shook his hand as well. She wished she knew what she could say to ease some of the hurt he felt, but what could she say? If she were in his place, there wouldn't be words to make her feel better. She whispered, "I'm sorry, Mike."

Mike's expression remained blank as he looked past her. "Me, too." He paused for a moment and took a deep breath as he scanned the long line of people still waiting to give their condolences. He patted her back. "Thanks for coming."

Melody made her way to Drew and their friends. Gracie grabbed hold of her hand and squeezed it. "It's awful, isn't it?"

Melody didn't know what to say. She simply nodded.

"Mike said he wasn't supposed to be out there." Wyatt's voice was low. "Their dad told him they didn't need to be out swimming that late."

Nick shook his head. "I guess Joe had been giving them a hard time lately. It can be awfully difficult being a young teenager."

"Yeah. We did some stupid stuff that could have landed us hurt—or worse," Drew added.

"But God protected us," said Nick.

Melody furrowed her brows. Then why wouldn't He protect Joe? She needed to go home and search the scriptures, to spend some time in prayer. Aunt Renee told her things would still happen that she wouldn't understand, but now that something *had* happened, she wanted to understand why. She looked up and saw that Drew was staring at her. He knew what she was thinking.

sixteen

Drew hadn't been able to have Bible study with Melody for a week. He'd spent a lot of time working, praying, crying, or simply being there for Mike and his family. They supported one another and spent a lot of time trying to bask in God's comfort, but they still struggled with Joe's death. He also spent a lot of time listening.

Today she was coming over. He'd missed seeing her, and he worried that Joe's sudden, unexpected death would cause her to stumble in her new faith. She already struggled with wondering why God allowed bad things to happen. Truthfully, *he* wondered why some bad things happened. Joe wasn't where he was supposed to be, but Drew couldn't count the times on all his fingers and toes that he and his buddies had gone swimming after dark, not to mention the times they'd disobeyed their parents.

"For the wages of sin is death. . . ."

He closed his eyes, remembering when he'd learned that *wages* didn't mean "penalty." It meant "payment." Growing up, he'd always thought the verse in Romans was saying that the punishment for sinning was to die, but that wasn't what the scripture said. It said the payment he received for sinning was death.

"But the gift of God is eternal life."

But instead of letting him die for all eternity, Jesus had

saved him. In terms of eternity, he was saved. God could have taken him the night he fell out of the fort he and his buddies set up when they were eight, after his mom had told him not to climb up in it. Nick could have died when he was a teenager and was driving his dad's pickup too fast in the rain. He hit a slick spot and slammed into a tree. They could have and should have died, but God had chosen to spare them.

He'd chosen to take Joe.

Drew let out a long breath and sat on the bench. He picked up his Bible and held it between his hands. Peering out over the amazing creation God had formed, he whispered, "I don't know why, but I have to trust You."

He placed the Bible back on the bench and stood and walked to the edge of the pond. He bent down and picked up a few smooth stones and skipped one across the top of the water.

He was nervous about Melody's reaction to Joe's death. For all Drew knew, she may not even show up for their Bible study. He feared she'd decide the whole faith thing wasn't worth it, because bad things still happened, and she couldn't control them.

Listen to me, God, I sound just like Melody. Here I am stewing about her. You're big enough to handle my worries and her worries, and the whole wide world's problems if we'd only give them to You.

He skipped another rock. It had been a hard week. It hurt to let Joe go. It hurt to watch Mike and his parents in so much pain.

But the week also confirmed for him that he loved

Melody. He didn't just care for her. She wasn't solely his friend. She was the woman he wanted to marry. He wanted to sit on these benches and read and study God's Word with her every night. He wanted to hold her close and to have her work hard alongside him. If she'd have him, he'd pack her up in his truck and take her wherever he could to marry her tonight.

He looked at his watch. Melody was nearly a half hour late for their usual Bible study time. *Then again, she may not show up.*

≈

Melody couldn't believe she was running so late. She'd missed seeing Drew something fierce all week. His friend and family needed him, and she'd never do anything to keep Drew from helping someone in need.

He probably thinks I'm not coming. She looked down at her greasy coveralls. She knew her hair was an absolute wreck. She'd always cleaned up before going to Drew's for their Bible study time. She'd even starting dabbing on perfume the last few times they met. Today, she simply rushed out of the shop and headed straight for his house.

AJ told her she didn't have to stay to help. It was after five, and he'd planned to just tell the woman to bring her car back in the morning. But when Melody saw the lady and her three small children waiting in the lobby and how tired the woman looked in her factory uniform, Melody simply couldn't make her come back the next day. She'd probably have to call in sick and lose money she most likely needed. All the car needed was a couple of new gaskets. It really didn't take her that long.

She looked at the clock on the dash of the truck. She was almost an hour later than usual. For all she knew, Drew may have given up on her and left. Her stomach growled. *If he's not there, I'm running through a fast-food restaurant.*

But she wanted him to be there. She needed to see him. A week without him proved to her how much he meant to her. He was more than her best friend. She loved him.

Through a lot of prayer and Bible study, she'd learned that a part of her may always have moments of fear when it came to men being bigger and stronger than she was. It was kind of like a scar from the experience she'd had. It was there, and sometimes she noticed it, but it wouldn't hurt or bother her unless she allowed herself to focus on it.

She couldn't change that her dad left her mom. She couldn't change that the man attacked her in the park. But with God's help, she could control how she reacted to the memories of those things.

She drove through the thick wooded trees and into the open field. She saw Drew's log house. He was living in it now, but he hadn't been able to take her on the official tour since he'd finished just before Joe's death.

Looking at the tree, their tree, she spied Drew standing beside the pond. He skipped a rock across it. She could tell he'd cleaned up for her, as he always did. He must have heard the truck because he turned, and if she saw right, he seemed to offer her a hesitant smile.

She snuck a peek in the rearview mirror. Just as she feared, she had grease smeared across her left cheek, and stray hairs clung to her temples and forehead from working all day.

God, help me not to be consumed by what I look like. I just want to enjoy seeing Drew and spending time in Your Word.

The night before she'd looked over the chapter they were going to study. It was 1 Corinthians 13. Her aunt had winked at her saying it was the "love" chapter. And it was. It talked of love being about patience and kindness. It wasn't proud or rude or angry.

The verse that stuck with her was verse seven. *"It always protects, always trusts, always hopes, always perseveres."* She'd gone to bed repeating the verse over and over in her mind. Drew had shown her that kind of love, and it made her realize just how much she loved him as well.

She parked the truck and jumped out. He was walking toward her, and she looked down at her coveralls once more. She noticed that even her hands were dirty. *I can't believe I didn't even wash my hands.*

"I thought you weren't coming." Drew's smile had deepened.

She swept her hand down the front of her coveralls. "I wasn't sure I would make it. A woman came in late needing some gaskets fixed, and I just couldn't turn her away. I know I look a mess." She lifted her hands. "I should have at least washed my hands, but I knew I was running so late, and I didn't want you to worry, and. . ."

She took a breath, realizing she was babbling. Her nerves were getting the best of her. She wanted to look pretty the first time she saw Drew again. *My thoughts have changed a bit, huh, God?*

She bit her bottom lip to hold back a smile. "I'm really glad I made it."

"Me, too." He lifted his hand and touched her cheek with the back of his hand. Her heart beat faster. "I missed you this week."

"I missed you, too."

At any moment she thought her heart might beat out of her chest. She wanted to scream out just how much she missed him, how much she loved him. She wanted to wrap her arms around his neck, and for the first time feel his lips pressed against hers.

He smirked, and for a second she wondered if he could read her thoughts. He picked at a patch of sweat-dried hair against her temple and wrinkled his nose. She noted the gleam in his eye when he said, "Would you like to clean up a bit?"

She lifted her hands palms first in front of him and acted as if she were going to wipe them on his shirt. He flinched, and she laughed. "Do I have to?"

He pointed to the house. "Yes."

She feigned a pout as she stomped onto his front porch and through the front door. The house looked beautiful. Just as she'd suggested, he'd bought dark brown leather furniture and accented with bits of red in the living room. She made her way down the hall.

"I'll give you a tour when you get out."

She turned to see Drew standing inside the front door. She nodded and walked into the bathroom. Turning on the water, she gasped when she caught sight of her full reflection. She really was a mess.

She scrubbed her face clean and pulled the ponytail out of her hair. She didn't have a brush, but she spied a comb on the counter. She couldn't get all the tangles out of the mass with just a simple comb, but she could at least make herself look presentable.

Unzipping her coveralls, she wished she'd worn something nicer beneath them. Of course that wouldn't make much sense when she had to spend eight hours a day working on vehicles. She sighed. *Oh well, the cutoff sweats and T-shirt will have to do.*

She sniffed under her arms and wrinkled her nose. She could seriously use some deodorant, and she wished she had her toothbrush. Spying men's spray deodorant on the shelf above the toilet, she giggled. *Should I use it or should I not?*

Not wanting to stink, she decided to take her chances on smelling like a man and sprayed a little on. *Maybe he'll think it's just from working with the guys all day.*

As presentable as she could get herself, she folded the coveralls over her arm and walked back into the living area. He smiled at her and winked. "Much better."

He sniffed the air. "Do I smell my deodorant?"

Warmth raced up her neck, and she shrugged. "At least I don't stink."

Drew smacked his leg, bent back his head, and laughed. "Melody Markwell, I really did miss you this week."

She laid the coveralls on the back of one of the wooden chairs around the dining room table. She loved how the house was so open. He'd made it so the living room and dining room and kitchen all shared one big area. The house was small, but the design made it seem so much bigger. "Do I still get a tour of the house?"

"Absolutely." He stood, and she followed him down the

hall. He pointed to the first door on the right. "You've already seen the bathroom." He opened the second door on the right. "This is the guest bedroom." She nodded at the room painted a plain white with nothing more than a bed and dresser inside. It definitely looked like a guy had decorated it, but then she liked simple. But maybe not that simple.

He turned and opened the door on the left. "Here's the master."

Not sure she felt comfortable going into his bedroom, she just peeked inside. Again, he didn't have pictures or any decorations, only a huge bed, dresser, and armoire that held a TV. But just as she'd envisioned and suggested, he'd put in french doors along the back wall. The simple brown curtains were open, and she could see they opened up to an enormous deck that was probably only twenty yards from the pond. "It's beautiful, Drew."

"Thanks. It means a lot to me that you feel that way."

A sudden wave of emotion washed over her. She stepped away from the door and walked back down the hall and into the living area. She looked back at the puzzled expression on his face, but unable to talk without crying, she walked outside the door.

She stared up at the sky. The sun still shone bright, and it was still hot and humid. Her stomach growled again, and she patted it to be quiet. *I love him, Lord. I love him. I want to tell him, but. . .seeing his house—I could imagine it being our house, his and mine.*

"Melody, what's wrong?" Drew stepped out onto the front porch.

Still unable to say anything, she sat on one of the porch swings and started to rock. She tried to look up at him and grew flustered again. She stood up and grabbed one of the poles and gazed at the wooded area in the front of his house.

"Melody?"

She smacked her hip. "Who would have ever thought I'd be so nervous?"

"Why would you be nervous?"

She spread open her arms and smacked them down on her thighs. "Because I love you. I love that you're God-fearing. I love that you're hardworking. I love that you're competitive, and that you're protective, and that you're my very best friend. I love the way you get sunburned along the base of your hair every time you get a haircut. I love—"

Drew wrapped his arms around her, and before she could say another word, he pressed his lips against hers. She inhaled and closed her eyes at his sweet touch. Feeling weak, she wrapped her arms around his neck. He pulled away, looked at her lips, then kissed her again, then again. She giggled when he pressed his lips to hers a fourth time.

"You have no idea how badly I've wanted to do that."

Melody unwrapped her arms then placed her hands on her hips. "I think you just wanted to kiss me before I kissed you."

He cupped her cheeks with his hands and kissed her again. "You're right about that."

He pulled her close to his chest and wrapped his arms around her back. She felt another soft kiss on the top of her head before he released her enough to lift her chin so that he could look into her eyes. "I love you, Melody."

She lifted her eyebrows and smirked. "I said it first."

"But I kissed you first."

"Oh yeah, well—well. . ." She searched her brain for a comeback. "Well, I'm going to ask you to marry me first."

"Oh no you're not."

Melody gasped when Drew pulled a small box out of his front shirt pocket. He bent down on one knee and took her hand in his. "Melody, I've been carrying this ring around with me for a month. I knew one day God would show me when I could give it to you."

Her heart beat so fast she thought it would take flight and soar out of her chest. He opened the box, and she gazed at the gorgeous marquis diamond. It was simple, just like her. It was perfect. "I love you, Melody. Will you marry me?"

Her hand trembled as he touched the ring to her fingertip. Unable to speak, she nodded, and he pushed it all the way up her finger.

A sudden wave of excitement surged through her, and she flung herself into him for a big hug. He lost his balance and fell backward. She toppled toward him, and they bopped heads.

He sat up and rubbed the place that was already turning red. "So this is how it's going to be?"

She laughed as she felt to see if she, too, had a bump forming. With her other hand she punched his arm. "Every day."

He reached over and pinched her nose. "I'll take it."

epilogue

May

Drew could hardly wait for the wedding to just start already. He'd been waiting all morning to get the thing going, and he was just about to lose his patience. He didn't care about all this fancy dressing up and the pink and yellow flowers and the white lace and whatever *else* they decorated the church with. Now the food afterward, he was okay with *that* part of this whole wedding gig. But all the froufrou stuff—he just wanted to make Melody his wife.

He already knew her long dark hair fell like perfect waves all the way down her back when she didn't knot it up in a ponytail. He already knew her eyes were the deepest, darkest brown he'd ever seen and that he could get lost in them. He knew she had the prettiest lips of any woman he'd ever known, and that she had a tiny, yet remarkably strong frame.

He didn't need to have a big old fancy wedding.

The music started. Finally. He cleared his throat and lifted his shoulders. At least she wasn't going to make him wait too awfully long to see her since she'd decided to just have Addy and Gracie as bridesmaids. It broke his heart that her mom said she couldn't make it to the wedding. He still hadn't met her in person, but he and Melody continued to pray for her every night.

Addy walked toward them first, and Drew blew out his breath. His sister had told them last night at the rehearsal that she and Nick were expecting their first child in six months. He snuck a peek at Nick. He'd always heard that women glowed when they were pregnant, but it was Nick doing the glowing. He shrugged. He supposed it would be nice to have a little niece or nephew.

Gracie walked down next. She was huge with her second child. She looked like she was going to pop at any moment, but God answered Melody's prayers with a yes. She'd prayed every day for months that her friend would wait until after the wedding to go into labor. And she had. Although if Drew were a betting man, and Melody told him she'd wring his neck if he did any more of that, he'd wager that Gracie would have that baby before they got back from their honeymoon. That had actually become Melody's new prayer, as she wanted her to wait until they got back.

Drew shook his head. Melody would be appearing next. He already knew she was beautiful. He'd tried to be supportive about the whole wedding bit, but if he'd had his way, they'd have been married the day after he proposed. And she could have worn her coveralls for all he cared.

The wedding march sounded, and everyone in the church stood. Melody and Roy moved from behind the left wall and into the center aisle.

Drew sucked in his breath. He couldn't remember how to let it out. She was an angel. She was amazing. Gorgeous. Stunning. Her long white dress didn't have any sleeves at all. It was simple, but it hugged her body to perfection, and

Drew felt light-headed that she was the woman God had given him to marry. A see-through material hung from the top of her head all the way down her back.

That beautiful hair of hers was all tied up in knots at the top of her head, but she had curls that framed her face and fell along her shoulders. But it was her eyes and her smile that absolutely blew him away. She looked at him as if he'd made her the happiest woman in the world.

He felt humbled that Melody would love a man like him. *God, You're too good to me.*

She and Roy finally reached him at the altar, and Drew took her hands in his. The ceremony went by so fast that Drew could hardly remember anything he said. The beauty of his bride and the fact that she'd allow him to be her husband mesmerized him. The only words he'd heard were "I do." They were the two best words he'd ever heard in his life.

"You may kiss your wife," the pastor said, and Drew's chest puffed up so full he thought it would burst.

He'd promised himself that he wouldn't embarrass her with a long, drawn-out kiss in front of all their family and friends. Her gaze was glued to his as he bent down and lightly touched her lips with his. He smiled and stood to his full height.

"Oh, I don't think that's good enough, buddy," Melody whispered. Gripping his shirt with her right hand, she pulled him down to her and kissed him with everything in her. Drew felt woozy when she let him go, and again he inwardly praised God for having this woman to deal with.

The pastor coughed back a chuckle. "I present to you Mr.

and Mrs. Drew and Melody Wilson." She squealed when Drew lifted her into his arms and carried her down the aisle. He could hardly wait to take her home.

He placed her on her feet at the front door of the church so they could shake hands with everyone as they left. Leaning over, he whispered, "I love you, Mrs. Wilson."

She lifted her chin and kissed his lips quickly. "I love you, Mr. Wilson." She kissed him again.

He growled. "You know I expect a lot of those tonight."

She cocked her head and smirked. "Betcha I can give you more kisses than you give me."

Excited anticipation filled him. "Now that's a bet I'd like to make."

A Letter To Our Readers

Dear Reader:

In order that we might better contribute to your reading enjoyment, we would appreciate your taking a few minutes to respond to the following questions. We welcome your comments and read each form and letter we receive. When completed, please return to the following:

Fiction Editor
Heartsong Presents
PO Box 719
Uhrichsville, Ohio 44683

1. Did you enjoy reading *Betting on Love* by Jennifer Johnson?
   ❑ Very much! I would like to see more books by this author!
   ❑ Moderately. I would have enjoyed it more if

   _____

   _____

   _____

2. Are you a member of **Heartsong Presents**? ❑ Yes ❑ No
   If no, where did you purchase this book? _____

   _____

3. How would you rate, on a scale from 1 (poor) to 5 (superior),
   the cover design? _____

4. On a scale from 1 (poor) to 10 (superior), please rate the
   following elements.

   ____ Heroine   ____ Plot
   ____ Hero   ____ Inspirational theme
   ____ Setting   ____ Secondary characters

5. These characters were special because? _____

_____

_____

6. How has this book inspired your life? _____

_____

_____

7. What settings would you like to see covered in future **Heartsong Presents** books? _____

_____

_____

8. What are some inspirational themes you would like to see treated in future books? _____

_____

_____

9. Would you be interested in reading other **Heartsong Presents** titles? ❏ Yes ❏ No

10. Please check your age range:

   ❏ Under 18   ❏ 18-24
   ❏ 25-34   ❏ 35-45
   ❏ 46-55   ❏ Over 55

Name _____

Occupation _____

Address _____

City, State, Zip _____

E-mail _____

CONNECTICUT WEDDINGS

When life hands them each a roadblock, three Connecticut women must choose how they will react to changes in their dreams and plans. Can Deena, hopeless; Celie, homeless; and Jamie, jobless, find new promises from God along paths of romance, or will the new men in their lives only add to their trials?

Contemporary, paperback, 368 pages, 5.1875" x 8"

————————————————————

Hearts♥ong

Any 6
Heartsong
Presents titles
for only
$20.95*

GET MORE FOR LESS FROM YOUR CONTEMPORARY ROMANCE!

Buy any assortment of six *Heartsong Presents* titles and save 25% off the already discounted price of $3.99 each!

*plus $4.00 shipping and handling per order and sales tax where applicable.
If outside the U.S. please call
740-922-7280 for shipping charges.

HEARTSONG PRESENTS TITLES AVAILABLE NOW:

(If ordering from this page, please remember to include it with the order form.)

Presents

Great Inspirational Romance at a Great Price!

Heartsong Presents books are inspirational romances in contemporary and historical settings, designed to give you an enjoyable, spirit-lifting reading experience. You can choose wonderfully written titles from some of today's best authors like Wanda E. Brunstetter, Mary Connealy, Susan Page Davis, Cathy Marie Hake, Joyce Livingston, and many others.

When ordering quantities less than six, above titles are $3.99 each.
Not all titles may be available at time of order.

HEARTSONG
PRESENTS

If you love Christian romance...

$12.⁹⁹

You'll love Heartsong Presents' inspiring and faith-filled romances by today's very best Christian authors...Wanda E. Brunstetter, Mary Connealy, Susan Page Davis, Cathy Marie Hake, and Joyce Livingston, to mention a few!

When you join Heartsong Presents, you'll enjoy four brand-new, mass-market, 176-page books—two contemporary and two historical—that will build you up in your faith when you discover God's role in every relationship you read about!

Imagine...four new romances every four weeks—with men and women like you who long to meet the one God has chosen as the love of their lives...all for the low price of $12.99 postpaid.

Mass Market 176 Pages

To join, simply visit www.heartsong presents.com or complete the coupon below and mail it to the address provided.